FATAL FESTIVAL DAYS

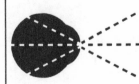

This Large Print Book carries the
Seal of Approval of N.A.V.H.

A DOG DAYS MYSTERY

FATAL FESTIVAL DAYS

JAMIE M. BLAIR

WHEELER PUBLISHING
A part of Gale, a Cengage Company

Farmington Hills, Mich • San Francisco • New York • Waterville, Maine
Meriden, Conn • Mason, Ohio • Chicago

LIBRARY OF CONGRESS CIP DATA ON FILE.
CATALOGUING IN PUBLICATION FOR THIS BOOK
IS AVAILABLE FROM THE LIBRARY OF CONGRESS

ISBN-13: 978-1-4328-6448-4 (softcover alk. paper)

Published in 2019 by arrangement with Midnight Ink, an imprint of Llewellyn Publications, Woodbury, MN 55125-2989 USA

Printed in Mexico
1 2 3 4 5 6 7 23 22 21 20 19

To Eddie, my little furry love.

ACKNOWLEDGMENTS

Thank you to every reader who joined me and Cameron in Metamora over the course of three books. I hold all of the Dog Days characters near and dear to my heart. This one is dedicated to you and your fuzzy friends.

ONE

The devil must be selling snow cones, because for the first time in a decade, the Whitewater Canal was frozen over.

Mayor Soapy Thompson scuffed his foot across the snowy bank. "Last time Metamora saw a winter this cold, everybody's pipes froze except Judy's and we all took refuge at The Briar Bird Inn."

The last thing I wanted to do was bunk down with the town. I made a mental note to dig around in the garage to see if Ellsworth House had a generator to keep the basement toasty and the pipes running. Seeing as how a century and a half's worth of junk had accumulated in there, my odds were good for finding one. Of course being in possession of a generator would mean the town would come knocking on my door. Good thing I had five smelly, poorly trained dogs that jumped on anyone who stepped foot inside, attempting to lick them to death.

Not that they were a great deterrent. They hadn't kept my mother-in-law away. Which reminded me, I still owed her a new blouse since hers was ruined by giant, muddy paw prints.

"We couldn't ask for better weather for the Winter Festival," I said, taking in the glittering ice and snow as far as the eye could see. "Do you ski, Soapy?"

"No, never learned. I do ice skate, though. Played a little hockey in my younger days." He eyed the canal with interest, scratching the scraggly white beard that hung to the collar on his coat. "Is it too late to add an event to the festival schedule? I think I'll get Roy down here to clear this ice for skating. Maybe a friendly game hitting the old puck around."

"I've already made the flyers, but you know how well word of mouth works around this town."

He smiled, his eyes gleaming with the prospect of using the ice. "That I do."

"Well, good luck finding Roy." *Sober,* I didn't bother to add. Everyone knew where to find Roy. The Cornerstone Bar, three sheets to the wind. I had to give Roy credit though — he and the rest of my Metamora Action Agency — they really pulled this festival together. It kicked off the next

10

morning, and for once, we weren't putting out last-minute fires.

Working for the town in an official capacity had been . . . interesting so far. The fall Canal Days Festival had had its obstacles. Notwithstanding murder and flooding, it ended up going off without a hitch. Planning the Winter Festival had gone as smooth as butter — which was worrisome.

I tried not to be a pessimist, but there's always a kink in the hose, so to speak. When there wasn't, I walked around waiting for the sky to fall on my head. If something bad would just happen, I could get past it and not look for it. It wouldn't be the specter on the horizon.

And this event was the biggest the town had ever had, at least the coverage — it was to be televised! A local Indiana station was covering the skiing and ice carving tomorrow afternoon and evening, and I'd managed to wrangle local Olympian David Dixon into hosting the events. David competed in the giant slalom in the 1972 games in Japan. He didn't medal, but he's still an Olympian, and that's as good as gold for hosting Metamora's own winter games!

I spotted Logan and Anna, two of my Action Agency volunteers, tacking up festival fliers in the town gazebo. They were one

11

pair of my four seniors, the two that were seniors by high school grade and not age. "How's it going?" I called to them, trekking over, my boots crunching through the shin-high snow.

The only advantage to having the world frozen was that my knee didn't give me grief like it did when it was humid and about to rain.

"Almost done!" Anna called back, her auburn hair tucked behind her ears under her hat. "We have a problem, though."

And there it was, the specter, come to haunt my festival. "What problem?"

"Paul Foxtracker and John Bridgemaker and their Mound Builders' Association are making signs," she said.

"Signs for what? Just drop the bomb. Rip the Band-Aid off. I can take it." I took a deep breath and squared my shoulders, prepared to face this obstacle.

"They're picketing the downhill skiing," Logan blurted through the scarf covering the lower half of his face.

"Logan!" Anna shouted, whacking him in the arm. "I told you I'd tell her."

Logan was brilliant and analytical. He got along famously with computers but wasn't one for dealing well with humans.

"Picketing the skiing?" I asked. "Why?

What do they have against skiing?"

"It's not the skiing," Anna said. "It's where the skiing is taking place. That hill is one of the earth mounds their ancestors built."

"Oh . . ." A hollow feeling sank into my chest. "That is a problem. Why didn't any of us know that? Is there a map or something of all the earth mounds? How did this happen? It's on Clayton Banks's private property. Wouldn't he know it's an earth mound?"

"He said he didn't think it was a big deal, and that it's his earth mound to do with what he wants," she said, frowning. "We've been trying to think of somewhere to move the event, but so far, I can't think of anywhere else."

"Clayton likes the prospect of the town paying him to use his land for the event and parking," I said. "I'm sure any thought about the earth mound and what it means to John, Paul, and the rest of the association members might have crossed his mind for a second, but the dollar signs would've cleared his conscience pretty fast."

Clayton Banks was a notorious swindler and tightwad. He'd do just about anything for a buck. Last week he tried to trade my sister, Monica, a dozen rusty cans of motor

13

oil for a lifetime supply of her homemade dog treats from her shop, Dog Diggity.

"I need to talk to Clayton," I said. "Anything else come up that I should know about?"

"Just Johnna —" Logan began, but Anna swatted him again.

"Nothing!" she said.

"Oh good gravy, what did Johnna do now?" I asked. She was the fourth member of my action agency, a senior in age, and had a proclivity for sticky fingers. She'd come to my group originally by way of the court system — service hours for stealing yarn. I was convinced she crocheted and knitted in her sleep. I'd never seen her without her needles clicking and clacking away.

"She may have gotten the Daughters of Historical Metamora all wound up about the dog sled races," Anna said.

The Daughters of Historical Metamora were a group of women whose ancestors founded the town. My mother-in-law, Irene Hayman, was their ring leader. When she wasn't doing everything in her power to drive me crazy, she was busy reclaiming her ancestral estate, Ellsworth House, where I lived, piece by piece. A weather vane here, a door knocker there. "What could the

Daughters possibly have against a dog sled race? Are they allergic to Huskies?"

Anna looked at Logan, who only shook his head. "It discriminates against cats," he said.

"I'm sorry?" I said. "What? I don't think I heard you correctly."

Anna winced. "Fiona Stein said you're always planning events that exclude cats. Your pro-dog agenda is discriminatory."

"Pro-dog agenda? Since when do cats pull sleds? This is insanity!"

"Don't kill the messengers," Logan said, adjusting his gloves to get a better grip on a tack.

"I'll just have to give her a piece of my mind. Discriminatory, my rear." I stomped off shouting, "Thanks for putting out the flyers!" behind me as I went.

Heading for the Whitewater Train Depot, which was owned and operated by Fiona and her husband, Jim Stein, I crossed the wooden bridge over the canal trying to calm down. I'd never been accused of being discriminatory in my life. How dare she!

I hit the other side of the bridge just as my husband, Ben, came running out of the Soapy Savant, the coffee bar that also sold homemade soaps owned by our mayor, Soapy, and his wife, Theresa. "Your events are a jinx!" he shouted spotting me.

"What? What did I do?"

He yanked open the door on his police pickup truck, Metamora One, and Brutus — his giant, black Rottweiler/Doberman mix — darted from behind him and hopped up in the cab. "Clayton Banks was just found dead at the top of that ski hill of yours."

Stunned, I ran toward him as fast as my Storm Trooper–sized snow boots would let me. "I'm coming with you!"

"Oh no you're not. You're always sticking your nose into these things —"

"And figuring out who did it!" I shot back. "You're welcome."

"And almost getting killed yourself," he said.

"I'll stay in the truck." I pulled the passenger side door open.

Brutus stuck his wet nose in my face and wouldn't budge from the seat. "Scoot over, you big slobbery —"

Brutus barked, indignant.

"That's an officer of the law you're talking to," Ben said, jumping in behind the wheel. Brutus had recently become an official K-9 officer and Ben's partner.

"Fine. Please scoot your furry hind end over, officer," I said, digging in my handbag

16

for one of Monica's newest treats, a Beggin' Bagel. "Here," I said, bribing Brutus with a snack.

"You don't give police dogs treats," Ben said. "Here, Brutus," he ordered, patting the spot in the middle of the seat. Brutus moved over. I climbed up and pulled the door closed behind me.

The siren blared and Ben rushed us across town, past the driveway to Clayton's house to the very end of his property, where orange snow fencing had been set up in his field to indicate the public parking area.

Food trucks and port-a-potties were abandoned in the middle of being set up, their workers gathered together waiting for Ben to arrive. A few members of the Mound Builders' Association stood by with their picket signs resting on the trunk of a silver car.

Ben grabbed his radio receiver and spoke into it. "Metamora One on the scene. Over."

"Brookville two minutes out. Over," came the reply. Officer Reins from Brookville PD would be arriving shortly. I'd had my experiences with Reins, seeing as how he made me a suspect in a murder last summer. This was Metamora's third murder — if that's what this was — in the past eight months. John Bridgemaker and Paul Foxtracker had been on the scene when the last body was found. Their luck was running about as well as my own. Maybe we shared the same specter.

I was beginning to think the events I planned for the town actually *were* cursed.

"Allen Henderson?" Ben called out, hoping down from the cab of his truck with Brutus on his heels. I rolled my window down to eavesdrop. I said I'd stay in the truck, after all. For now, I'd keep my word. No promises though when Ben was out of sight.

"I'm Henderson," a man said, striding up. "I'm the one who called."

"Take me to him," Ben said, meaning Clayton.

The whine of more sirens reached my ears. An ambulance and two police cars skidded into the makeshift parking lot, light bars flashing.

Ben waved the paramedics to follow him. Reins ambled out of his cruiser, tugging up his police belt and holster. He headed toward the group of workers and stopped beside a man I recognized — by his white handlebar mustache and shiny bald head — as a school crossing guard who stood at the corner down from my house. I didn't know the man's name, but I thought of him as

18

my nemesis.

Did people have nemesises (nemesi? nemeses?) or was that only a thing in movies? Regardless, he'd yelled at me for stopping to wait for a kid on a bike and not taking a right-hand turn when he'd waved me on. The last thing I needed was to plow over a kid on a bike. When I did turn past Mr. Mustache, I did something I probably shouldn't have and gave him a certain finger gesture to show my annoyance. Since then we'd traded glares and scowls whenever I passed his corner in the afternoon. Mornings are not my thing.

I got out of Metamora One and strode over to Reins, Mr. Mustache, and the group of festival workers. "Mrs. Hayman," Reins said, "this is a police matter. Not a wife of a police officer matter, no matter how many cases you claim to have solved."

"Claim to have solved? I don't need to claim to have solved them, I did solve them. We both know it. So what's the story here, fellas?" I asked the group. "I know you," I said to Mr. Mustache. "You're a crossing guard by my house. What are you doing here? Port-a-potty patrol?"

"Directing them where to set up, yeah," he said. "What of it? I know you too, lady," he said. "You're a troublemaker. Maybe you should listen to the officer and butt out."

"Hey!" I said. "That's not very nice."

"I didn't think you cared about nice, Miss Middle Finger," he said.

"That's enough," Reins said. "This is an official crime scene. Mrs. Hayman, unless you have a statement to make, please return to your husband's truck."

I was about to protest when my eyes landed on John Bridgemaker's white SUV pulling in. "Fine. If you need me, you know where to find me."

I didn't know the men with the signs mulling around the silver car, but I hustled over as John parked beside it. "John," I said, as he got out, the beaded fringe on his leather vest swaying. "I heard about the issue with the mound. I had no idea. I'm so sorry."

"Guess it's not an issue anymore," he said. "There will hardly be a downhill skiing event now."

"Right," I said, just realizing the full implication of this situation. Pushing the panic aside — I'd worry about the festival later — I concentrated on Clayton's death. "Did you speak with Clayton today?"

"Briefly." John shook his long black hair behind his shoulders. "He called and told me to get my goons and their signs off of his property."

Goons? Well, that wasn't neighborly at all. Not that I had anything to say about nice, apparently, since I'd been dubbed Miss Middle Finger. "What did you say?"

"I told him we had a constitutional right to protest. These mounds were made by our ancestors. They aren't here to be desecrated for the town's entertainment."

"I had no idea. I hope you believe me."

"I figured Clayton hadn't mentioned it."

"No, he hadn't."

We both turned our eyes toward the top of the hill. "I know what they'll think," John said.

"You didn't do it. I know that. Ben knows that."

"And Reins? He kept me in jail in Brook-ville for the last murder in this town until *you* figured out who really did it. I happen to have a good motive to be a suspect this time as well."

The last time, John and Paul had been trying to purchase Butch Landow's farm for a casino when Butch ended up dead. This time John has a quarrel with Clayton and Clayton ends up dead. "It does seem to be a pattern," I said.

"So you do think I did it?"

"No! Of course not."

"Who then? One of those guys?" he asked,

21

nodding toward his friends with their signs, leaning against the car.

"I don't know them, so I can't say. But I'm sure Reins and Ben will want to talk to all of you."

"I know the drill," John said.

Just then I spotted a disturbing sight. Two paramedics were walking back down the hill with a stretcher between them, a body-bagged figure strapped on top. "Good gravy," I whispered. "How did this happen?"

My cell phone rang in my handbag. I'd recently ditched my organized bag with pockets hidden behind zippers and snaps, for my big, old, reliable bag where every-thing sat in a jumble at the bottom. As dif-ficult as it was to find things in my jumbled mess, it was easier than when I was orga-nized.

I dug around for my phone in the bottom of my bag, dredging up a candy bar, a travel sewing kit, and a tin box of breath mints before finally finding it. The caller ID showed Soapy. I had a feeling he'd heard about Clayton. Like I'd told him earlier, word travels fast in this town.

"Not to sound insensitive, but what can we do?" he asked. "We have a television crew and an Olympian coming tomorrow morning."

"I'll think of something," I said. "Don't worry. And I know you're not insensitive."

"Have the police contacted Clayton's son?"

I knew he'd had one kid. Ben had gone to school with him. I didn't know his name or where he lived, only that he was an adult who'd left Metamora.

"I don't think they've gotten that far yet." The paramedics loaded Clayton's body into the back of the ambulance. The coroner hadn't yet arrived.

Ben eyed me from across the yard with a shrewd expression that silently told me to hustle my way back to Metamora One, close myself up inside, and stay out of police business.

These cops were all alike: didn't think they needed help from anyone.

"We need to regroup and make a plan," Soapy said. "Get your team together and I'll meet you at your house in an hour."

"Sounds good. I'll see you then." I hung up trying to shift gears in my brain from Clayton's death and possible murder to finding a different event and getting people to compete in it before morning.

It was going to be a long, long night.

Two

The dogs were extra rambunctious. It was like someone had told them I was having an important meeting and they should be wild beasts.

"Cross-country skiing!" Anna shouted, and wrote it on the white board with a squeak of smelly dry-erase marker. A master of organization, she'd brought her own whiteboard and easel from her bedroom.

Gus, my giant Newfoundland, barked his approval at the suggestion while my nameless duo, the twin terrier tanks who I'd been toying around with naming after famous TV twins, chased each other around our feet, barking their pint-sized brains out underneath my kitchen table.

"My yarn!" Johnna cried, as one brownish tank darted out from between her ankles with a ball of pink yarn in his mouth that she'd been using to make a teapot cozy.

"Nicky!" I yelled, getting up to chase him

down the hall but tripping over Isobel, the senior canine in my pack, a crabby German Shepard. She snarled and growled at me. "Don't look at me like that," I told her, "you never stray from beside the fridge. How was I supposed to know you'd be sitting by the back door?"

The second twin monster took chase. "Alex! You two get back here!"

"Nicky and Alex? Let me guess. *Full House?*" my sister, Monica, said, following the yarn trail toward the front door. "I'll get them. You get on with brainstorming."

"This place is a circus," Roy said out of the side of his mouth to Soapy, then took a swig of whatever was in his flask — most likely moonshine, the specialty of Old Dan, town patriarch. Soapy accepted the flask when Roy offered and took a long drink, wincing as he swallowed.

"Where would we put the cross-country ski course?" Logan asked Anna, ignoring the antics going on around him.

"I don't know, Logan," she said, snottily. "You think you know everything, so what's your idea?"

Good gravy, a teenage love quarrel was not what I needed right now.

"I know!" I said. "I'll see if we can use Landow Farm." After being chased by a

25

murderous duo around that farm myself not long ago, I knew the sloped land would be perfect. "Let me call Phillis."

Phillis Landow had ended up owning the farm after her ex-husband was murdered. She was a cantankerous old bat who, I knew, would only let us use her land if I owed her a favor of ten times the magnitude at some point in the future. But, seeing as how I had few hours left to come up with an alternative and was almost to the point of selling my soul, Phillis seemed like the ideal fiend to come to terms with.

I grabbed my cell phone off the counter and hurried into the dining room, sliding the pocket door closed behind me for a bit of privacy. "Phillis!" I said with the most warmth and enthusiasm I could muster when she answered. "It's Cameron Cripps-Hayman. I have a favor to ask you."

"Of course you do. A town shindig can't be pulled off without me being pulled in, can it? What is it this time?"

I let her attitude bounce right off me and plunged forward with my request. "Well, you may have heard about the tragedy that happened this morning. Clayton Banks was found dead on his property."

"Shame," she said with no feeling behind the word. Did the poor man not have one friend who would mourn his passing?

"Yes, it is a shame. The thing is, it puts the town in a real bind since we were going to use his land for downhill skiing."

I swore I heard her chuckle. "What a mess for you. I hear there's a TV crew coming and you have that old Olympian, Dixon, hosting and everything. What will you do to pull this off?"

"I'm hoping that's where you come in."

"Me? What on earth for?"

"We'd like to use Landow Farm for a cross-country ski course to replace the downhill event."

"Oh, I see." She hummed and I pictured her drumming her fingertips together as she contemplated how to best use this scenario to her advantage.

"The event would take roughly four hours and since your farm butts up to the center of town where there's plenty of parking and room for vendors to set up, it seems like a perfect solution."

"Perfect for you maybe," she said. "But I have to put up with all those people on my property. With people comes trash and cigarette butts, destructive teens trying to break into my barn and harass my cows, kids climbing my trees and breaking the limbs. No, no. I don't think I can allow it."

Soapy opened the dining room door and stepped in. "How's it going?" he whispered.

I shook my head.

"Let me talk to her." He held out his hand for the phone, and I handed it over.

"Phillis, dear, it's Soapy. The farm's looking as good as ever."

Whatever she said, he closed his eyes and stroked his white beard.

"Yes, I'll get right down to business," he said. "The town will pay you for the use of your land and . . . yes, an hourly rate . . . yes, cleanup included, and what?" His brow creased. "I'm not sure we can . . . well, yes, we want to use . . . okay, okay," he said, turning weary eyes to me. "We'll let you cohost the event on television with David Dixon."

"What?" I shouted. "No!"

"Yes," he hissed, covering the phone with his hand so she couldn't hear him. "We're up against a wall and the clock, Cameron. We do it this way or there will be no event."

"Oh, it's going to be a nightmare," I said under my breath.

Soapy made the final arrangements with Phillis as I slumped back into the kitchen.

"She said no?" Anna asked, her face dropping from hopeful to defeated.

"Of course she did," Johnna said, looping

her yarn around her hook. "That crotchety old bag wouldn't let a starving person have a ham bone from her trash."

"She agreed," I said, plopping down in my chair at the table.

"What did you agree to, Cameron Cripps-Hayman?" Roy asked, eyeing me suspiciously.

"Nothing. Soapy did the negotiating."

"And?" Johnna asked. "How much damage?"

"She cohosts with David Dixon."

Roy started laughing so hard he snorted. Johnna whipped her yarn around, crocheting a chain at the speed of light, muttering something about how she should be the one to cohost if any old person could do it. Logan turned to Anna and started to say something, but she held out her hand, stopping him. "Not a word," she said. "You didn't have a better idea, did you?"

My Action Agency was coming apart at the seams. "Okay," I said, slamming my palms on the tabletop to get their attention. "Granted, this isn't ideal, but it's what we have to work with. Look on the bright side, we have an event! We still have David Dixon. We still have TV coverage. We'll deal with Phillis. It's going to be okay. No, it's going to be great! The greatest event we've

29

put on yet. And beggars can't be choosers, right?"

They all nodded, reluctantly.

For better or for worse, this festival was kicking off in the morning, and Phillis Landow was now a major part of it.

A little after five o'clock, Ben came into the house with my stepdaughter, Mia, on his heels. "Want me to order a pizza for dinner?" he asked. "Assuming you don't already have plans," he added.

We'd been separated for about a year, but we spent more time together now than we had when we were living together. Overall, marriage to Ben was better when he lived in the gate house at Hilltop Castle and I stayed here at Ellsworth House, his ancestral home. When we spent time together now, we were actually present in the moment and not just in the same room.

"That would be great," I said, sending off a quick text message to Soapy reminding him to meet David Dixon at the mayor's office in the morning. "I have a ton of little ends to tie up tonight."

"I can help. I'm good at taking orders."

"You're good at giving them, copper."

He laughed and gave me a peck on the cheek.

"Dad, you have to take me to the school, remember? I'm cheering tonight!"

"Oh. Right," he said. "What time was that again?"

"I have to be there in an hour!" Mia's hands shot to her hips and she stormed up the stairs.

"Guess I'm on my own for dinner, huh?" I said.

"I'll come in when I drop her off after the basketball game and see if you're hiding under the dining room table."

"You know me so well," I said.

Actually, I was getting better at managing the stress of living in a small town full of quirky characters who seemed to live to throw a wrench into every well thought out plan I put together.

"Monica home tonight? Or is she off with Quinn?"

"She's off with Quinn, and has been every night. I hardly see her anymore."

My sister and her boyfriend, Quinn Kelly, a former K9 trainer in Scotland, and new owner of a training facility/kennel up the road in Connersville, Kelly's K9s and Kennels, had become inseparable in the few months they'd been together.

Ben's phone rang. "Hayman," he said, answering, and held up a finger to me to give him a minute. "Yeah . . . Okay . . . Thanks."

"What was that about?" I asked as he hung up.

"Clayton's cause of death has been determined. Don't ask what it is. It's not being released to the public yet."

"I'm not the public. I'm your wife." I knew this argument would get me about as far as a bike with no wheels, but it was worth a shot.

"I don't believe for one second that after I walk out of here you won't be on the phone with everyone you know and be aware of the cause of death before Clayton's family is told."

"Don't blame me because your law enforcement pals blab. If they didn't love to gossip, I'd never find out."

"Law enforcement officers don't gossip. I can't speak for everyone in their offices, though."

"It's a small town, and not everyone keeps information from their wives."

"I do," he said, punctuating it with raised brows and a stiff upper lip.

"I know. I get nothing out of you. It's a waste of having a husband who's a cop."

"I'm a waste now?"

"For information? Yes. Overall . . . I suppose not."

I laughed, and Ben chuckled. "Good to know," he said.

I grabbed a pack of Monica's freshly baked dog treats off the counter and tossed them to him. He caught them and looked over the packaging. "New kind?"

"Dogs Dig Banana Bonanza," I said. "Let me know if Brutus likes them."

"That's Captain Brutus to you," he said.

"Oh, did you promote him? Does he have a team of K9s who report to him now?"

"Not yet, but I'm working on it."

"Good gravy. That's just what this town needs. More bossy dogs."

After Ben and Mia left, I grabbed the phone and called Andy Beaumont, town documentarian, my handyman and one of my loyal friends, even if he was only twenty-two.

"Hey, Cam, what's up?" he answered. "Let me guess, you're having a panic attack about tomorrow morning. Well don't. This festival is going to go off without a hitch. We've made sure —"

"Clayton Banks is dead," I said, stopping his claim of things going smoothly this time around. Andy and his girlfriend, Cassandra Platt, the owner of the Fiddle Dee Doo Inn, had gone up to Indianapolis for the day to do some shopping. I figured they hadn't heard about the murder.

"Banks is dead," he repeated, and I heard Cass say, "You're not serious!"

The phone rattled on Andy's end and then Cass spoke. She'd taken it from him. "Cam, how did this happen? When? I dropped off some flags to mark the ski course just this morning before we left for Indianapolis! He was fine!"

"You saw Clayton this morning? What time?" I grabbed a pen and notepad from my junk drawer to write down what might be my first clue to figuring out what happened.

"A little after eight. Andy and I wanted to get to the mall around nine so we'd have all day to shop."

"You mean you did," I heard Andy say. I couldn't imagine him spending an entire day in the mall. Then again, he'd do anything for Cass.

"He answered the door and I went inside for a couple minutes. He was drinking coffee and eating toast and was the same as ever. What happened to him?"

"He was found at the top of the ski hill," I said. "Or what we were using as a ski hill but turns out is an ancient Native American

34

mound. The police are treating it as a homicide."

"A homicide! Another one?"

The phone rattled again and Andy came on. "How was he killed, Cam?"

"That's what I don't know. Ben was just here and got a call telling him the cause of death, but of course he's not going to tell me."

"Of course not, but after the last murder in town, I did some interviewing and filming at the medical examiner's office. Let me see if I can find out anything."

"It pays to have a documentarian as a friend," I said.

"It pays to *be* a documentarian in this town. I'm thinking of shifting the premise to true crime since everyone keeps getting themselves whacked."

"You've been watching *The Godfather* again, haven't you?"

"You caught me. I'll do some digging and call you back when I have some info."

I hung up feeling antsy. I wanted to start questioning everyone in town, but I had a million little things to get in order before morning.

However . . . We would need the flags Cass dropped off at Clayton's house for our cross-country course. It probably wouldn't

35

hurt to just drive over and see if anyone answered the door.

There was a car in the driveway when I pulled up at Clayton Banks's house, and a light was on inside. As I made my way up the sidewalk, each hesitant step was taken in doubt.

I shouldn't be here, I told myself, but took one more step.

It's too soon. What will I say? But again, I kept moving forward.

Until I got to the porch steps and reality hit me. A man died this morning. Whoever was inside was grieving, and I had no business being on their doorstep.

I turned and took two quick strides before my boot caught on the pole of a shepherd's hook on the edge of a flower bed, tripping me up on the icy cement and sending me careening into the Barberry bushes.

My handbag went flying. I cried out as thorns poked me from my cheeks to my shins. The more I moved to get free, the more the prickers caught on my coat.

I was vaguely aware of the porch light flickering to life and the front door squeaking open. A dog was barking to high heaven. Then someone was grasping my arms and tugging me free and up on my feet.

Through the snow-covered hair flopped across my face, I made out a man of about my age glowering at me. "What are you doing out here?" he asked, then turned to a red bear-like dog on the porch. "Quiet. Sit." The dog obeyed, but scowled and showed her teeth, threatening me to watch myself. The dog could only be Clayton's Chow Chow, Ginger.

I tried to smile while brushing snow from my face, but I really needed a box of Band-Aids from all the cuts inflicted by the evil bushes. If only I knew where my bag had landed.

"I'm sorry to bother you," I said. "My name is Cameron and I'm in charge of the winter festival that kicks off in the morning."

"Well, it won't be happening here," he said. "In case you haven't heard, my father was murdered."

"I know. I'm so very sorry. My husband is Officer Hayman, our town's policeman."

"Officer Hayman who refuses to arrest that Indian who poisoned my dad?" He took a step forward, his expression going from angry to downright menacing. "You have a lot of nerve showing up here. A lot of nerve going through with this festival when it's the reason my father was murdered." His chin lowered so his eyes could glare at me at a better angle, and his hands clenched into fists.

I didn't know what to say, so I fumbled for words. "I understand how you must —"

"No, you don't understand!" he roared. "You're in charge of this festival and you're going through with it. You're making a mockery of a dead man! You'll be sorry, Cameron," he threatened, spitting out my name with venom. "You'll pay for going through with this. Now get out of here before I remove you myself."

He didn't have to tell me twice. I spun around scanning the bushes for my purse. It lay overturned on the sidewalk, everything inside scattered in the snow. "I just need to gather my things. They all spilled. It'll just take me a second or two."

Who was I kidding? I'd be there until midnight searching around in the half-dark through snow and ice. I hustled — very aware of where my boots were landing this time — and knelt beside my collection of bric-a-brac.

The door slammed shut behind me, and the porch light went off, leaving me in darkness. Even moonlight was shut out by the dark clouds threatening more snow. I scrambled around searching blindly for my wallet and cell phone; anything else wouldn't be the death of me to leave behind. My hand grasped something round and I shoved it in my purse. My wallet was a few inches away, and my cell was a little farther down the sidewalk. Good gravy, I hoped the screen wasn't broken.

After finding several more items, a few of which I vaguely identified as a tube of lipstick, a pack of gum, an empty sunglasses case, a nail grooming kit, and a bottle of travel-sized shampoo, I threw my bag over my shoulder and hightailed it to my car. Actually, it was Monica's car since Mia totaled mine a while back and I hadn't replaced it, but that was neither here or there.

I jumped in and started it up, hit reverse and got out of there as fast as a four-cylinder hybrid engine could take me. I always teased Monica that she drove a wind-up toy, but it had some power and got me out of there in a hurry.

Good gravy, I was panting like I'd gone ten rounds with Mike Tyson. Clayton's son sure had a temper! I couldn't hold it against him, though. He was shocked from the news of his father's murder and grieving. I'd have to make due without the flags marking the course. We'd figure something out. The Action Agency always came through in a pinch. I might not have gotten the flags, but I left with something more valuable. Information. The cause of Clayton's death was poisoning.

THREE

I spent most of the night awake, attempting to focus on the little last-minute details for the festival, but finding my mind wandering in circles trying to think of anyone who might poison Clayton Banks. And how?

Standing at the top of the cross-country course at Landow Farm with the early-morning sun glittering across the snowy fields, we were an hour away from our first event. Johnna was stringing bubble gum pink yarn between tomato stakes that Roy had pounded into the frozen ground as substitute course markers for the flags I wasn't able to retrieve. Logan was tapping away on his laptop keyboard while Anna berated him for making the Excel spreadsheet to track the scores for the event in a way she deemed totally wrong. I needed to set aside some time to talk with her. She was behaving so differently from her normal analytical but easygoing self that something had to be wrong. Poor Logan was taking the brunt of whatever it was.

"Get into a cat fight?" asked my best friend, Brenda Fields, looking at the scratches on my face as she walked up next to me.

A mauve toboggan hat covered her hair, which she always wore in a bun with a lace doily pinned around it. She wore matching mittens and a scarf with Johnna's initials knitted on a corner. Anything Johnna made these days, she wanted the world to know she'd crafted.

"Barberry bush fight," I said. "It looks worse than it is."

Looking past me, her jaw dropped. "It looks better than that."

I turned to see what she was talking about and almost fell over getting an eyeful of Phillis Landow in a fur coat spotted black and white like a cow. Like a Dalmatian. I gasped. "She's Cruella de Vil."

Brenda's wide eyes gleamed and she grinned. "I've never seen a more realistic imitation of a cartoon character. I didn't know you were putting on the Ice Capades."

Phillis was arm-in-arm with David Dixon, my Olympian. His old wool coat looked moth-eaten and like it had gone a few rounds with a greasy towel, but he was who we had on offer. I reminded myself again that beggars couldn't be choosers. Anyway, he was a nice, older gentleman who represented our town well. I was just being judgmental because I was panicked about this festival going off well in front of television cameras.

"No, no, not them too," I said, spotting the Daughters of Metamora getting out of their Cadillacs and Lincolns with picket signs.

"*Cat-A-Strophic Speciesism?*" Brenda said, tilting her head as if she'd read my mother-in-law, Irene's, fluorescent yellow sign wrong. "What's speciesism?"

"This can't get any worse!" I threw up my hands in surrender.

"Now, it's not that bad." Brenda patted my shoulder trying to console me.

"Not that bad? A) I have Cruella de Vil as a spokeswoman. 2) Johnna and Roy are stringing pink yarn as course markers. And thirdly, I have the newly founded cat cartel picketing the festival. The local TV station will be showing up any second!"

"Okay, okay. It's not the best situation. I'll go deal with the Daughters and call Soapy and Theresa for backup. You focus on the event."

Soapy and his wife would get Evil Irene

43

and her minions to back down. The last thing the Daughters of Historical Metamora wanted was to make their town look bad.

I took a deep breath and tried to refocus. "Thanks for your help. It'll be okay. It'll be great."

"That's the spirit." She gave me a thumbs-up and headed toward the group of women who were determined to make my life impossible.

I knew they were doing this to get back at me for refusing to repaint Ellsworth House white again. Well, I wouldn't. I'd had more compliments on the sea green and lavender that I'd ever had on my white house.

I headed down the slope toward Cruella — I mean Phillis — and Dixon. Phillis's bright-red lipstick shown like a beacon against the white backdrop of snowy fields. "Morning!" I called, waving. "The announcer's booth has coffee and donuts if you —"

"Don't be silly," Phillis said. "I've brought a catering crew in from Brookville for the VIPs who will be happy and warm in a heated tent on the first turn in the course. Great angle for the cameramen," she said, nodding at Dixon with a *cat who ate the canary* smile on her overwaxed lips.

"You've gone to such trouble," he said,

44

patting her hand. "I hope this last-minute change in events didn't put you out too much."

I wanted to throw snowballs at them both. "That was very nice of you," I said instead. I mean, who was I kidding? It was nice. It was something I didn't have the money to do. Heck, the coffee and donuts stretched my budget. I just wished it wasn't something for her to hold over my head. I pictured a little yellow feather poking out of her mouth and I was the canary she'd gobbled down.

"You go on ahead and make sure the skiers know what to do and where to go," she said, giving me a little shove. "David and I will greet the camera crew." She turned to Dixon again. "Did you know they're sending their top reporter to cover the festival? Ed Stone."

"Ed covered my story back when I competed in Japan," Dixon said. "He was at the airport with his cameraman when I got home."

They continued their chat as they hiked up toward the parking area, leaving me to wonder who was in control of this festival. Clearly not me. It was becoming obvious that I had to let this first event fall into Fate's hands and hope for the best. It was a Hail Mary anyway. The main goal was keeping Ed Stone from reporting on Clayton's murder more than the festival coverage.

"Wait!" I yelled, chasing after Phillis and Dixon. "Wait a minute!"

They stopped and waited for me to catch up. "Do us all a favor and steer Ed Stone away from any idea of talking on camera about Clayton's death. That's the last thing we need."

"Oh, psh." Phillis waved me off. "It'll make Metamora more interesting. More urbane and sophisticated."

"Three murders in less than a year isn't sophisticated!" I said, trying not to shout even if I couldn't keep my voice from raising hysterically. "The focus will shift from something good — the festival — to something bad — a town of under two hundred people with a murder problem."

Phillis literally clutched her pearls. "When you put it that way, it does sound wretched. Are we in danger, Cameron? Should I sell the farm and move out of Metamora? I don't want to be killed!"

"Please tell me you're not serious," I said. "This is no time for these questions."

"That's two percent," Dixon told her. "Two percent of the town's population has been murdered in the last eight months."

"Two percent," she repeated, whispering

with terror-filled eyes. "And one my dear ex-husband, Butch."

"Anyway," Dixon continued, hooking his arm through hers and resuming their journey uphill, "it's a terrible time for real estate sales. Nobody wants to buy in a murder town."

Murder town? Fabulous, our celebrity host was calling Metamora a murder town. It didn't seem like there was any way to keep a lid on those two. Unless . . .

I jammed my hand into my bag, searching for my phone. The screen had been unscathed in its slip and slide across Clayton's sidewalk, thankfully. Something in my bag sounded like a maraca or a little container of Tic Tacs, neither of which should be residing in my purse.

I found my phone and dialed Andy. "Where are you and Cass? I need help."

"Is this a genuine distress call from Cameron Cripps-Hayman, Metamora Wonder Woman?"

"Don't play games with me. Where are you?"

"Walking over now from Fiddle Dee Doo. What's up?"

"I need you two to stay close to Phillis and David Dixon. Make sure they don't talk to the TV reporter about the murder."

"Why are you letting Phillis anywhere near the reporter?"

"What?" I heard Cass cry in the background. "We're on our way, Cam!"

"We're on our way," Andy repeated and hung up.

If Andy couldn't keep the conversation with Phillis and Dixon on track, Cass would spellbind Ed Stone by batting her beautiful blue eyes at him.

My phone rang. Soapy's number showed on the screen. "Thank goodness," I said, answering. "Are you and Theresa helping Brenda keep the Daughters under control?"

"They want a cat competition," he said.

"A cat competition? Like what? A race climbing the snowiest tree? What do I do with cats?"

"I don't know, but you better think of something. Elaina Nelson's passing out headbands with cat ears. Their protest is gaining support. People like cats, Cam."

"I like cats, too." Elaina Nelson was the oldest person in town and battier than — "Soapy, what is that I hear?"

In the distance I could just make out a raspy, deep male voice over a loudspeaker, chanting, "Metamora's gone to the dogs!"

"Old Dan's got the CB radio in his pickup hooked up to a blow horn on top of the cab.

You know Elaina's got him wrapped around her finger these days."

The two oldest people in town were the hot new couple on the block. Old Dan and Elaina, or El Danaina as Mia liked to call them. She said it was their celebrity name, combining their two names into one that sounded like a Mexican resort to me. Or maybe a Mexican old folks home, since it was Dan and Elaina.

"Fine," I said. "Tell them I'll have something indoors featuring cats. I'll call Irene tonight. Just get them out of here!"

"Will do. Oh, and Roy, Old Dan, and I have the hockey tournament all figured out. You don't have to do a thing."

"Perfect. I won't."

I hung up. The last thing I wanted to do was worry about a hockey tournament when I had a spontaneous cat fiasco to put on.

I checked the time. Thirty minutes until this event was to start, and I had no idea where any of my skiers were.

I marched over to the starting line, where Anna and Logan were still bickering. "What time did you guys tell the contestants to be here?"

They both fell silent. Their eyes tracked back and forth to each other and to me a few times. Logan's fingers flew over his keyboard and he turned his laptop screen toward me. "We weren't assigned that task. Our task list for this week includes hanging flyers, meeting at your house for an emergency brainstorming meeting, and adjusting the score sheet in Excel from downhill skiing to cross-country skiing. Each has been confirmed completed."

"Some more poorly than others," Anna said, spurring their debate to start again.

"Wait!" I held up my hands in a T for time out. "Are you telling me nobody told the skiers not to go to Clayton Banks's house?"

"That doesn't sound like something you'd put Johnna and Roy in charge of," Anna said, tucking a strand of fiery red hair behind her ear. "So, if we weren't asked to tell them . . ."

"Oh, for the love of all that's good and gravy! Someone call Monica and get her over there diverting people over here. I'll call Ben to help."

Anna wasted no time dialing Monica's number on her cell phone while I got Ben on mine. "I have a serious emergency," I told him.

"Have you called 911? We've talked about this before, Cam —"

"Ben! Not that kind of emergency."

"What other kind is there?"

"The kind where I forgot to tell the downhill skiers to come to Landow Farm and not Banks's place."

I heard the siren on Metamora One blast to life. "On my way," he said and hung up.

"Monica and Quinn are heading to Clayton's," Anna reported back to me.

"Good, thanks. Between them and Ben, hopefully we can get the skiers over here before the television crew starts to wonder where they are."

And hopefully before Clayton's son went ballistic finding them on his property.

"Cam, I have bad news."

I knew that tone from Ben. Firm but gentle. He wasn't someone to let you down easy. He was more the rip off the Band-Aid type. This was going to be bad, bad news. "I don't want to know," I said. "Just make it go away."

"Sheriff Reins is here at Banks's. He's arresting the skiers for trespassing. Jason Banks, Clayton's son, was waiting with his phone in his hand to call the cops if anyone stepped on his property. And there's something else. He said to tell you this was what he said you had coming, and if you continue to go on with this festival there will be hell to pay. You want to tell me when you talked

51

to him, Cam? When you talked to him, and he threatened you and you didn't think it was a good idea to tell me — your husband and the town's only law enforcement officer?"

This was worse than bad. Now Ben was involved. "It wasn't a big deal. I went over there last night to get my course markers. He wasn't pleased that we were going through with the festival after his dad was murdered. That's all. I understand why he's upset."

"I don't like him doling out threats, especially not to my family. You should've told me."

"We can discuss this later. Right now I have a cross-country ski competition without skiers! The TV crew will be here any minute!"

"Sounds like you better strap on a pair of skis, Cam." He hung up, still in a huff. I stared at my phone. He'd get over it. He always did.

"Emergency Agency meeting!" I shouted. Anna and Logan were standing two feet away from me.

"You don't have to yell," Anna said. "I'll call Johnna and get her and Roy over here."

"Okay," I said, feeling a little chastised by

Miss Snippy. Logan shot me an apologetic look.

Roy and Johnna shuffled their way through the snow, Johnna using a tall walking stick and wearing boots with treads so big I didn't know how she lifted them off the ground. Roy didn't even wear a winter coat, just his everyday navy sport coat that had to have been purchased sometime during the seventies, which was most likely the last time it was clean.

"What's the good word, boss?" Roy asked.

"No good words, Roy. We have a huge problem. The skiers went to Clayton Banks's and got arrested for trespassing. We need to round up some of our neighbors to compete."

"Our neighbors are old!" Johnna said, winding her pink yarn into a ball. "Get your sister and Mia."

"What about Andy and Cass?" Roy asked.

"I'll ask them. You four come up with some other names and start dialing."

"What about you?" Anna said. "Logan and I can compete, and I'm sure you can cross-country ski at least enough to get to the end of this course."

The last time I raced through Landow Farm, I ended up tail over teakettle chasing a killer. I wasn't eager to repeat the trip. "I

53

will if it comes to it," I said, noncommittally.

"It's your festival," she said, shrugging with a smirk.

"You and I need to talk," I said. "Later."

"You're not my mom." She turned and stomped off.

"This day is going so well." I jabbed Mia's cell phone number on my screen.

"Do you know how early it is?" she asked, answering with a groggy voice.

"Not very. The whole town is at Landow Farm getting ready for the first event. I need your help. I'm in a serious bind."

She groaned. "Fine, but I'm getting a trip to the mall out of this. A real mall. Not the strip mall in Brookville."

"Deal." I told her I needed her to ski and after some haggling about new boots we came to terms. "Grab Stephanie on your way. You both can ski." Stephanie was Elaina Nelson's youngest great-granddaughter and Mia's best friend. I knew I'd end up lugging her along to the mall with us anyway, so I might as well get some skiing out of her, too.

Next I got Andy back on the phone. "I need you and Cass to ski. I'll explain later. Come to the starting line." I wasn't giving them the option to say no. I'd do it for them, and I'd most likely end up doing it for myself.

"Cam!" Monica called, slogging through the snow toward me. Quinn was right beside her. "We were too late. Reins was already there when we got to Clayton's."

"How can we help?" Quinn asked.

"Can you two ski? I need to replace my contestants. Do they ski in Ireland?" I asked Quinn.

"Of course! I'm not great at it, but I'll give it a go."

"Do you have skis?" Monica asked.

"I brought the skis," Ben said behind me, scaring the daylights out of me. I spun around, startled. "I figured you'd need them, so I asked everyone who was planning to compete if I could borrow their skis for whoever you got as subs. Not like they could take them to jail anyway."

"You really are a hero," I said, as his phone rang.

"Hey," he said answering. "Pick you up? Mia, I can see the house from here." He shook his head and walked, back toward his truck.

"Okay, we've got Mia and Stephanie, Monica and Quinn, Anna and Logan, and Cass and Andy. That's eight."

"This course really isn't big enough for

very many, anyway," Johnna said. "It gets pretty narrow after that first turn into the trees."

"I'll run and give the news to Phillis and Dixon before Ed Stone gets wind of what happened." I hurried across the snowy field toward the tent at the first turn, getting wafts of bacon and waffles as I neared. My stomach rejoiced, but I told it not to get excited. There was no time for breakfast.

I broke into the tent just as Ed Stone was going on-air with his first live promo of the events to come. "I'm live in Metamora," he said into the microphone, flashing his brilliant white smile for the camera, "the little town known for its music, merrymaking, and now murder. We'll be back at the start of their first Winter Festival event. Back to you in the studio, Martha."

Panic exploded in my chest. *Music, merrymaking, and murder.* That's what he'd said. On live TV.

Good gravy, there was no recovering from this. The event had been hijacked by something more newsworthy happening in town. There was a murder to sensationalize. Jason Banks would have my head for this.

"None of the skis fit Logan," Anna said, crossing her arms.

56

"I have large feet," he said, hanging his head.

My substitute skiers had all made their way into the tent, lured by warmth, food, and problems for me to try to solve.

"I have skis, but no boots," Monica said. "Skiing was never a pastime of mine."

My mind whirled. I caught their complaints in my ears, but my thoughts were still stuck on Ed Stone's broadcast. "Phillis!" I called. "Can I talk to you for a moment, please?"

"Isn't it exciting?" she said, rushing over. "Our town, the center of mysterious murders that will capture the imagination of the nation! That's what Ed Stone said. The murders happening here will capture the imagination of the nation." She splayed her hands out in front of her, fanning her fingers through the air while stars danced in her eyes. "We'll be famous!"

Soapy threw back the tent flap and stormed inside. "This is a disaster, Cameron. How could you let this happen? We have no choice but to cancel this event." He ran a hand up over his white beard to his flaming red face into his snowy hair. "We'll be the laughing stock of the state!"

I closed my eyes, counted to ten, and took deep breaths.

Who was I kidding? I could count to a million and still not be calm.

"Attention, everyone!" I shouted. "Attention, please!"

Ed stone motioned to his cameraman to start taping.

"Due to circumstances that have arisen, we'll need to cancel this first event and resume this evening with the ice carving. I apologize for any inconvenience this causes. I'd like to thank Phillis Landow for her hospitality, and for allowing us to use her farm. We'll see all of you tonight beside the old Grist Mill, where we'll witness the best ice carvers this state has to offer, right here in Metamora."

Ed Stone rushed over and shot his microphone in my face. "Is this event canceled due to the grisly murder of Clayton Banks, owner of the property where this first event was originally slated to take place?"

"I wouldn't call it grisly," I said, looking around for help. Where was Ben when I needed him?

"Do you have information about the murder then?" Ed asked.

I wasn't even sure the police had made it known that it was a murder. "No. Why would I have — no."

"But it was in fact a murder? You can

confirm that much?"

"I can't — ask the police for a statement. My business is this festival. I hope everyone will join us this evening —"

"So you're not concerned about a possible serial killer on the loose in your town threatening the lives of festival goers?"

Ed Stone was on my very last nerve now. "Serial killer? What on earth leads you to believe that Clayton was murdered by a serial killer?"

"So it's verified. Clayton Banks was murdered."

"No! I didn't say —"

"You said he was murdered. How? There has been rumors of a disagreement between Mr. Banks and the Mound Builders' Association. Are they to blame for his murder?"

I looked to Soapy, pleading with my eyes for him to intervene, but he was shocked silent and still, frozen like he himself had been carved from ice.

Finally, Dixon took the microphone from Ed Stone and stepped in front of the camera. "Now, now," he said. "Let's not get ahead of ourselves. Just allow the police time to investigate the matter. Once they know more, I'm certain they'll release an official statement." He gave his golden boy smile to the camera, the one that had captured the hearts of every redblooded American back in 1972. "In the meantime, we invite everyone in the area to come out to the Grist Mill tonight for hot chocolate, music, and ice-carving demonstrations. It's sure to be fun for all!" He dropped the mic to his side and the cameraman stopped recording.

"What do you call that?" Soapy, who'd suddenly snapped back to life, asked Ed Stone. "Certainly not responsible reporting."

"Murder does wonders for ratings," Ed said, patting Soapy on the back. "You wait and see how many show up tonight just because it's the mysterious murder town."

"Don't say that again, I'm warning you." Soapy's expression was lethal. He pivoted and left the tent.

Slowly, my hodgepodge of skiers followed suit, pushing the tent flap aside and heading off for home. After Monica exited, she stuck her head back inside. "Cameron, you have to see this."

"What is it? An avalanche? I don't want to know."

"Nothing like that. Come look." She was smiling, so I figured it couldn't be all that terrible.

Outside, once news had spread that the cross-country event had been canceled, the kids in town had grabbed their sleds and made their own use of the course. "Where did they all come from?" I hadn't seen this many kids under twelve in the nearly five years I'd lived in Metamora. "Phillis is going to have a cow."

"Not on camera, she won't." Monica pointed to Andy with his camera, recording the whole thing.

"This is what the TV crew should be filming." I turned to find Ed Stone filling a plate over at the caterer's table. "Ed, there's something wonderful going on outside. You'll want to get it on tape."

"What's that? Unless it's another murder, I'm eating."

I wanted to mess up his dark, slicked back hair and choke him with his perfect Windsor-knotted tie. "The town kids have come together to use the ski course for sledding. In the wake of tragedy, the youth are keeping everyone lighthearted. That's a news story. A feel-good story."

"It's weak. Only the sensational stuff can get on the radar these days." He chomped into a sausage link as I kept myself from shoving his face in his plate. There was no reply that could be uttered without using words that would make a sailor blush. So I kept my trap shut and strode away.

It turned out Ed's cameraman followed me outside, took up a spot beside Andy, and started rolling. At least one of the professionals from the TV station had good taste in news stories.

Soapy and Theresa brought giant thermoses of hot cocoa from the Soapy Savant and passed out steaming cups to the sledders and their families. There was a reason Soapy had been mayor for so long. He truly cared about the town and the people who lived here. Many were like family to him and Theresa.

The first festival event might have been canceled, but this was the true story of Metamora, coming together in times of need with comfort and cocoa.

FOUR

"You know, Cameron Cripps-Hayman," Roy said, sidling up next to me through the crowd getting cocoa, "we have a few hours until the ice carving. Time enough to start digging into Clayton's murder."

"And don't bother telling us we shouldn't," Johnna said from beside him. "We've heard it before, and it's never stopped us or you."

"That's right," Roy said. "Don't be hypocritical."

Anna and Logan popped up on my other side. "I've made a list of Clayton's known enemies," Logan said.

"They didn't all necessarily want to kill him, Logan," Anna said.

"I never said they did."

I ignored the troubled teens, and turned back to Johnna and Roy. "I wasn't going to say that. I mean, it's true. We shouldn't get involved, but of course we will. We've proved our ability and would be doing Clayton's family a disservice if we didn't try to find his killer."

"It's decided then," Roy said. "I'll just pop home for a quick refill," he patted the flask in his inner jacket pocket, "and we'll meet in one hour in the church basement."

The church basement was our lair. We'd been forced out of it at times, like when I was a suspect for murder, myself. But we always ended up back in that damp, musty basement.

"Let's just head over now," Anna said. "You can go without alcohol for a couple hours."

"Blaspheme," Roy muttered.

"Everyone will think we're regrouping for the festival," I said. "It's the perfect cover."

"Something good comes from this debacle after all," Johnna said, "And here I was betting on the hockey match being the only saving grace."

Ignoring her jab, I led the way toward the bridge over the canal. If anyone wondered where we were headed, nobody stopped to ask.

Much to my horror, Mr. Mustache was shoveling the church sidewalk. "What are you doing here?" he asked. "I would never place you in a church."

"I could say the same for you. Anyone who yells at a woman for not plowing over a kid on a bike —"

"What are you saying? That kid was nowhere near crossing the street when you were at the intersection. You —"

"That's enough now," Johnna said, stepping between us.

"That's right," Roy added. "We've got important Action Agency business to discuss. If you'll excuse us, sir." He nudged Mr. Mustache out of the way and opened the door, holding it for the rest of us to enter.

"Thank you," I said, once we were all inside. "I don't know what that man has against me."

"You seem to bring it out in people," Johnna said, holding on to the railing and taking each step down carefully. "Speaking of which, I hear we have a cat competition to plan."

"Thanks to you," Anna shot back. "If you hadn't got those women all riled up about the dog sled race, we wouldn't have this problem."

"I don't know what bee's gotten into your bonnet, missy," Roy said, holding up a finger to her, "but you best respect your elders."

"There's no bee in my bonnet," she said. "I'm just sick of all of this." Once again, she turned and stomped off, shoving past Logan and back out the door, slamming it shut behind her.

"Logan," I said, "what's wrong with her? It's so out of character for her to act this way."

"She's stressed out. She has to decide which college she's attending, and should've done it months ago."

"She's usually so decisive about things."

"She's letting emotion dictate. She refuses to go by pros and cons alone."

"I see." My little robot, Logan, was off to MIT in the fall. It had been his destination since he was old enough to build with Lego blocks.

Downstairs, Johnna lowered herself into one of the old-school desks we used. "Kittens in mittens!" she shouted.

Roy shook his head. "What in the name of John Wayne's boots are you talking about, woman?"

"The cat competition, you old coot. We'll do something with mittens since it's a winter festival."

"You want to stuff cats into mittens?" he asked.

"Just their paws. Little kids mittens. The

66

last cat to keep them on wins."

"What if they all keep them on?"

She tilted her head and pressed her lips together, giving him a look that could sour milk. "Do you even know the first thing about cats? They hate having anything on their paws."

"Fine," he said throwing his hands in the air. "The cat problem is solved. We'll do the mitten cats, or whatever it was you called it."

With that out of the way, I proceeded to tell them what I knew. 1) Clayton was poisoned. B) Cass saw him that morning and he was just fine. And thirdly, Jason Banks was to be avoided at all costs, or we'd end up in jail with the skiing trespassers.

"Poisoned," Johnna said, pondering the idea. "What type of poison?"

"I've got Andy on the case. He's got a friend who works for the medical examiner."

"Clayton was down at the Cornerstone yesterday trying to talk Carl Finch into trading him a year's worth of chicken dinners for a year's worth of wheat flour."

Johnna began knitting. "That man was always trying to wheel and deal."

"And always with stuff nobody wants," Roy said. "What on earth would someone want with a year's worth of wheat flour un-

67

less you were a baker."

"I wonder if he tried to trade Betty for something," I said.

Betty Underwood, Cass's grandma, owned Grandma's Cookie Cutter, the bakery a couple doors down from my house and the reason I could stand to lose twenty pounds.

"I'll add it to our list of leads," Logan said, typing away on his laptop.

"Betty isn't a lead though," I said. "She had no reason to want to poison Clayton Banks."

"We don't know that," Roy said, waving a finger at me. "We can't dismiss suspects because they're friends of ours."

"She's not a suspect. We don't even know if she talked to him about this wheat flour."

"Fine, a lead then, but everyone is a potential suspect, Cameron Cripps-Hayman," he said, eyeing me suspiciously.

"I suppose you think I had a motive?"

"Time will tell. Time will tell."

"Roy," Johnna said, shaking her head, "you're as slick as sandpaper, you are."

"You just keep to your knitting over there."

"Who do you have down as an enemy, Logan?" I asked.

"The obvious at the top of the list — John Bridgemaker and —"

"Paul Foxtracker," I said. "I don't think

they're our killers. It's too obvious. And they're not murderers, anyway."

"Everyone's a potential suspect," Roy repeated.

"Who else?" I probed, nodding to Logan.

"That's all so far."

"Well that wasn't a long list."

"Not yet," he said.

"Nobody liked Clayton Banks," Roy said, sneering at the thought of the deceased man. "He was crass and dirty and a no-good swindler."

"Did you kill him, Roy?" Johnna asked, pulling a loop through with her needle.

"Nah, but I'm not upset he's gone neither. I'm man enough to admit it."

"What do you think happened to him?" I asked.

Roy leaned back in his chair. "Well, he wandered up on top of that hill and keeled over now, didn't he?"

"Who do you think would've poisoned him?"

"Maybe his own kid to get that house and land. Do we know when his boy showed up? Had he been there all along?"

"I don't know. Logan —"

"On the list," Logan said, tapping away on his keyboard.

"Good deduction, Sherlock," Johnna said,

poking Roy in the side with her knitting needle.

"Every now and then the old noggin churns up something worth thinkin' on," he said, tapping his head.

"First thing's first since we can't get into his house. I'll talk to Betty."

"I'll see what I can find online about Jason Banks," Logan said.

"And I'll stop home and get a well-earned nip of hooch," Roy said, grinning from ear to ear.

By that evening, Ed Stone's live broadcast was the talk of the town. Walking through the crowds to the Grist Mill, I overheard the phrase *mystery murder town* more than a few times.

"I'd like to ring Ed Stone's neck," I said, slamming my handbag on the counter inside the mill. Old Dan and his son Frank Gardner, made a bunch of hmm-ing and hawing sounds, but generally ignored my outburst.

"We're all set up over here in the corner," Johnna said, waving me over to a desk behind the counter where Logan sat with his laptop. "We'll tally the votes for the best sculpture, and get them all typed into Logan's machine here so nobody will think we cheated somehow or added them up wrong."

"It's a laptop," Logan told her for the two-hundredth time.

"It's also a machine," she said, clasping her hands and raising her brows in challenge.

"In the most basic definition, yes."

"Basic works for me," she said.

"Where are Roy and Anna?" I asked.

"Roy's out schmoozing with the crowd," Johnna said, "and we haven't seen Anna yet."

"She'll be here," Logan said. "Her controlling nature won't allow her to miss it."

"Well said," I told him. "I'm going to go take a look outside."

The ice sculptures were amazing. The sculptors had been working on them since that morning, and were etching in the final details. There were elaborate Disney characters, bold sports team logos, a gigantic 3D snowflake, and a ballerina that even spun on her ice pedestal. One of the sculptors had given an introductory class and the proud novices stood beside their chiseled ice snowmen.

The white lights strung up all over town cast a fairy-tale shimmer over the sculptures, giving the whole scene an aura of excitement.

The Soapy Savant was doing a booming business selling their coffee and tea, and Betty, who I hadn't yet had a chance to talk to, had made magic window cookies that looked like stained glass just for tonight. Kids and adults alike were oohing and aahing over the sculptures, debating which was the best.

This moment was what planning events for the town was all about. This was the reward at the end of the long days and weeks of preparation. I strolled through the crowd and took it all in.

I found Roy standing with Phillis and David Dixon. Phillis had undergone a costume change for tonight's event and was wearing a flowing blue velvet coat with rhinestone buttons. She looked every inch the ice queen. I had to hand it to her, it did add to the festivities. Dixon even got into the act, wearing a sequined silver top hat.

"You both look fabulous this evening," I said, bubbling over with cheer. "Have you picked your favorite yet?"

"I thought I'd take one more turn around the lawn and look them over again," Phillis said. "Care to join me, David?"

"Hmm? Oh, no, you go on ahead." Dixon

was scowling at his cell phone. "I think I'll hit the little boys' room before this thing really kicks off and Ed Stone makes his appearance. I'll catch up."

"All right," she said and wiggled her fingers at him, leaving us in a wake of blue velvet.

"Excuse me," Dixon said, and trotted off toward the facilities.

Roy angled his head toward me, and whispered, "Keep your eyes peeled. Everyone's a potential suspect."

"Right. I'll just go in and see if Anna's shown up yet."

Old Dan and Frank were sitting in rocking chairs on the mill's wide side porch that was added for tourists, sipping a hot beverage that I suspected was spiked with moonshine. "How's those bees, Cameron?" Old Dan asked.

Last fall Old Dan helped me relocate a colony of honey bees that had taken up roost in my porch column. They now resided in my yard in a bee box Dan built just for them.

"All balled up in a cluster like you told me they'd do."

"I'll be 'round to sing 'em a song."

"I'm sure they'd like that," I said. Old Dan insisted that bees had to be talked to and sung to and kept company or they'd swarm. I sat outside and practiced playing my clarinet until it got too cold.

Who was I kidding? I did it until the whole town complained about the noise and Ben made me stop.

I hadn't completely given up the clarinet, but I put my lessons on hold while planning the festival. There was only so much time in a day. Anyway, Fiona Stein, who gave me lessons, suggested I take up a different instrument, like the triangle.

I can admit, the clarinet wasn't exactly my forte.

Back inside the mill, Johnna startled when she saw me, and a pile of papers on the counter that she'd been perusing scattered in all directions. "What are you up to?" I asked her. Knowing her tendency to help herself to anything not nailed down, it was easy to jump to conclusions.

"Come look at this!" she whispered with a rasp, holding up a sheet of paper.

I crossed to the counter and took a peek. It was an order from earlier in the week for Clayton Banks to have a load of wheat ground into flour. She'd clearly been snooping under the counter.

"Where would he get that much wheat?" she asked. "And why?"

74

"That's a good question. I'm not sure it's tied to his death, but at this point, anything could be."

"Might have been poisoned," Logan said, not taking his eyes off his laptop. "Others could die, too, if they eat it."

"We're all going to die from wheat flour poisoning!" Johnna cried, throwing her hands to her chest and heaving breaths in and out like she was going to hyperventilate.

"No, we aren't," I said, guiding her into a chair. "Stop jumping to conclusions. This is just one fact we've gathered about Clayton's last week. It doesn't mean this has anything to do with his death. We don't even know if he ate any of it. Last we heard he was trying to trade it to Carl Finch."

"We need to find it and test it," Logan said. "I'll put that on our list."

"Good idea. In the meantime, we have an ice sculpting contest going on. Let's enjoy the evening and we'll circle back around to this after the festival is over. Did you tell Irene about Kittens In Mittens?" I asked, hoping to divert her mind away from being poisoned to death.

"No, I haven't. I'll go find her. She'll want to know right away."

I helped Johnna up and she scuffled across the floor to the door where she'd propped her exceptionally tall walking stick. "And I need to tell Monica," she added, turning back to me, "that my darling Charlie loves the Beggin' Bagels."

Johnna's darling Charlie was a rescue greyhound who had gone by the racing name Good Luck Chuck in his past life. Retirement was treating him well, curled up by Johnna's fireplace with a whole wardrobe of knitted and crocheted dog sweaters.

"He'll have to try the Banana Bonanza," I said.

"No, no. My Charlie's not fond of banana."

After she'd gone, Logan swung around in his swivel chair at the desk. "We need to get into Clayton's house. What do we know about his son, Jason? He had virtually no online presence, which isn't normal."

"Other than he's mean and wants the devil to rain down torment on me and this festival? Nothing."

"How old is he? If you had to guess."

"Early to mid-thirties."

"What kind of a guy does he look like? Is he rugged or sporty? Does he have a beard or wear khakis?

"I've seen him once. I think he had on jeans. I didn't get a good look at him. It was dark and I had snow all over me and I was bleeding."

"Bleeding?"

"I slipped and fell into a pricker bush by his front porch last night." I pointed to the scratches on my face. "Remember I said he wouldn't give me the flags? It was a whole thing."

"It usually is."

"What's that supposed to mean?"

One side of Logan's mouth cocked up into a grin. Was he joking with me? Mr. Literal himself, joking? Did he and Anna trade personalities or something? Not that Logan was ever grumpy. "So what's going on with Anna?" I asked, since my brain landed on the topic.

"Like I said earlier, she's stressed about college."

"It doesn't seem like her, though. Why is she having such a difficult time deciding?"

"Don't ask me. She was asking me a week ago if she should apply to Harvard."

"Harvard? Isn't that in Cambridge? Like where MIT is?"

"It is." He nodded.

"And? What did you tell her?"

"I told her it was a little late to be applying to an Ivy League school for the fall."

It was all too obvious what Anna's dilemma was, but Logan was oblivious. I shouldn't have been surprised, but I was. For a smart kid, he sure could be dumb.

"Logan," I said, trying not to shake my head in dismay, "have you and Anna talked about your relationship and what will happen when you go to MIT and she goes to wherever she ends up?"

He blinked about a million times, eying me like I was suggesting he launch into space without any oxygen — jump off the high dive with no water in the pool. He was way out of his comfort zone and about to short circuit. "Don't freak out," I said. "I'm not suggesting you propose or anything insane like that. I'm just asking if you've had a conversation with the girl?"

He shook his head. His fair complexion turned all ruddy, and I feared he'd break out in hives. I started digging in my bag for hydrocortisone. I kept it around for just this reason — the boy was prone to breaking out in hives.

"All right. Calm down. It's something you might want to do. She's probably not stressed as much as frustrated and confused that you don't seem to be concerned about the future of your relationship with her and if there is one."

"Should I be?" he asked, completely sincere.

"Should you not be?" I asked back. "I realize you're only eighteen. There's no need to get tied down to a long-term, long-distance relationship, but since you're in one now it's probably a good idea to talk about what happens after graduation."

"That's logical," he said, fanning his face with his hand.

"Can you do that?"

"I think so."

"Without a trip to the emergency clinic?" I shot him a smile, hoping for levity before this conversation killed him and he never made it to one with Anna.

"I know I'm not good at social conventions," he said. "I don't know what she sees in me. I never know what to say or how to act, or even what I'm supposed to be feeling."

I reached over and patted his knee. "Just be you, Logan. She likes you for her own reasons, just like you like her."

The Whitewater train blew its whistle, slowing on the tracks outside the mill and squealing to a stop in front of the depot. Air shot from the breaks and steam hissed. There was a lot of commotion and noise outside as a crowd of people disembarked from the train.

But the whistle kept going long after it

should've stopped.

"What is that?" Logan asked, his eyes narrowed suspiciously.

"The train whistle?"

"That's no whistle," he said.

The door flew open, banging as it hit the wall and Johnna burst inside. "Someone's screaming by the port-a-potties! David Dixon's dead!"

I shot out of my chair. "What do you mean David Dixon's dead? He's an Olympian! He can't be dead!"

"That has little to do with the fact that he's dead!" she shouted.

It was Phillis who was screaming. As I ran outside the mill, I caught sight of Carl Finch leading her away from the scene of the . . . of the port-a-potties. With Logan and Johnna on my heels, and Roy falling in behind them, we marched toward the apparent site of death, about ten yards behind the Fiddle Dee Doo Inn.

Ben was already there, with Andy and Jefferson Briggs, the owner of Court House Antiques, keeping people back from the crime scene.

And based on the blood spattered on Dixon's sequined top hat and the ice pick protruding from the top of his head, it was most definitely a crime scene and another murder. "That's two in as many days," I said. "They have to be related."

"What would Dixon have to do with Banks?" Roy asked. "Like water and oil, those two."

"That's what we have to find out."

Ben caught my eyes and shook his head, knowing what we were up to. He might not be a fan of the Action Agency, but he couldn't dispute our track record. We might not be conventional in our approach, but we could solve a murder — or even two.

FIVE

I took a sip of my coffee and plucked a second chocolate chip cookie off of the plate I'd set in the middle of my kitchen table. The Action Agency minus Anna had adjourned to my house to get our facts straight.

"When Dixon excused himself from Roy and me and went toward the port-a-potties he was upset or angry about something on his phone. He was texting or emailing, replying to someone's message."

"That's right, he was," Roy said with a bit of a slur, pointing at me. His flask had been a permanent fixture in his hand since sitting in his chair. If I didn't know better, I'd say Dixon's murder had shaken him.

It shook me, too. The image of that sparkly hat with the blood . . . I just prayed no little kids saw any of it. "Poor David," I said. "He was such a nice man. So charming."

"He was quite an athlete back in his day,"

Johnna said, wistfully. "I used to sit on my porch and wait for him to jog by just to get a glimpse of him in those little running shorts."

"Now you can't see past the bottom of your porch steps," Roy added. "A fella could streak right past your house in his birthday suit and you would be none the wiser."

"At lease I can blame my age for my poor eye sight. You're always pigeon-eyed from the booze," she said.

He held up his flask in salute and drank.

"Back to the facts," Logan said, always one for keeping us on track. "Where is Dixon's cell phone now? Did anyone see it at the scene?"

"No," I said. Roy and Johnna shook their heads in unison. "I'll ask Ben if he found it."

"Do we know who had an ice pick?" he asked next, going down a list he'd typed.

"Son, it was an ice carving competition," Roy said. "They all had ice picks."

"Do you know that for a fact? Every single competitor had an ice pick?"

"Of course he doesn't know that," Johnna said.

"Since the rest of the festival has been canceled, we'll start calling the ice sculptors in the morning," I said. "Ben took my list of competitors to question them, but I know who was there. We'll say we're making sure they have all of their tools and equipment and nothing was misplaced during the commotion."

"I have their names and contact information," Logan said. "I'll assign us each a list to call tomorrow."

"Don't tell me how to live my life," Roy said, taking another sip.

"We're heading into the belligerent drunk phase," Johnna said. "We better wrap this up before he passes out at your table, Cam."

"Roy, why don't you have a cup of coffee and I'll drive you home?" I said.

He waved me away, and stood on wobbly legs. "I'm fine to walk." He took two steps, stumbled, and fell into the wall, knocking down an antique framed drawing of the first Ellsworth House Thanksgiving done by one of Ben's many ancestors.

"I'll drive you," I said again, more insistent this time.

Logan was on his feet trying to help Roy back onto his, but Roy wasn't having it. "I may be an old man," he was saying, "but I'm plenty able to stand on my own!"

Johnna had her yarn bag all packed up and was struggling with her coat, getting wound in about seven feet of monogrammed, knit scarf and turning over the plate of cookies.

Logan's phone rang in the middle of the melee. He took a couple steps back from Roy who was swinging his arms now to free himself from any assistance, and answered. "I assume you heard about the murder."

Right to the point. No greeting, no small talk. That was Logan.

"We're fine." He dodged Roy's arm with a grunt. "*Fine* being a relative term. Nobody's hurt. Yet. Roy's drunk, and Johnna's throwing plates around, so I should say we're the same as always."

"Is it Anna?" I asked, holding the left side of Johnna's coat up for her to slide her arm into.

He nodded and spoke into the phone. "We're at Cam's getting ready to leave."

"Tonight?" he asked her. "It's getting late. No, if it can't wait, I — I'll see you soon then."

He hung up and tucked his phone back in his pocket. His face went pale and long, like it was drooping, or melting. "What is it, Logan?" I asked.

"I think she's breaking up with me. I've got to go."

He swiped his laptop off the table and strode toward the front door. I wanted to call to him, tell him something encouraging, but I found I didn't know what to say to a teenage boy facing his first breakup. Before my mind could land on something, he was pulling the door shut behind him.

"He's never getting over that," Roy said. "I'll get him a batch of hooch to numb the pain. Works wonders."

"He'll get over it just fine," Johnna said. "He's a smart boy, unlike you, you old gaffer."

"Takes one to know one," he muttered back.

It took some doing, but I got them both out the door. It was frigid, and I didn't want Johnna walking home, especially with a murderer on the loose. "I'll drop you off first," I told her, opening the passenger side door.

"I better sit in the back," she said. "You'll want him in the front with you to keep an eye on him. Make sure he doesn't pass out or get sick."

The last thing I needed was for him to pass out. I'd never get him out of Monica's car. I figured Roy getting sick was a long shot since he was always drunk. His body was in its natural state.

The roads were icy, but deserted. The whole town was home behind locked doors, wondering who on earth would want its only Olympian dead.

We crossed over the frozen canal. The Soapy Savant was shut up tight, and the lights were out in Read and ReRead. But over the bookstore, Brenda's bedroom light was on and I knew she was tucked in bed perusing a mystery novel, wondering about our town's latest victims.

"How were Clayton Banks and David Dixon tied together?" I mused aloud.

"They were inseparable back in school. Starnes Buntley was the third in their trio of friends," Johnna said without pause. "Those three did everything together. I used to baby-sit Starnes when he was just a boy. His wife inherited the family farm and they moved out to a farm by Hamilton, Ohio, about thirty years ago now."

"Wonder if anyone's told him what happened."

"I imagine someone has. He and Lana will probably come into town for the funerals."

"Maybe we should take a drive out there and make sure he knows," I said. "He might take it better coming from you since you knew him as a boy."

Who was I kidding? I wanted to find out what he might know, who he thought might want to murder his two friends.

"Guess we could take a drive over tomorrow," she said. "Betty was close with Lana's mother, and like a second mom to Lana. They're related in some way, I don't recall how. On Betty's husband's side, I believe, God rest him. She might want to go along. I'll give her a call."

"Good idea." I parked in the alley beside Johnna's house and noticed her porch steps were cleared. "Who shoveled your porch?"

"Andy always makes sure it's done. Cass better keep that one. He's a good catch."

"He sure is," I said. No matter how many grand ideas Andy had of leaving town and making big films, I had a feeling his roots had grown right down into Metamora's soil.

I waited until Johnna got inside with her door locked behind her before heading back across the bridge. "Where do you live anyway?" I asked Roy, who was staring out the car window and staying oddly silent.

"Over yonder," he said, nodding straight ahead. "Mike's disappeared."

"Metamora Mike?" I asked to make certain we were talking about the town's duck who lived in the canal with his harem of feathered females.

"You know another Mike?"

"What do you mean he disappeared?" I searched to the right and left, looking in the canal and around its banks.

"What does *disappeared* mean? He's gone."

"Maybe he flew south since the canal froze."

"Mike never flies south. He never leaves town. Not once in all the years I've been alive has Mike left town. He sleeps in the horse stalls, but he hasn't been seen since the canal froze."

The draft horses that pull the canal boat, the *Ben Franklin III,* from the banks were kept in stalls across from the train depot, alongside the canal when they weren't busy lugging it through the water.

I never knew Metamora Mike bunked down in their hay at night when they were back on their farm in a cozy barn.

"Where would he be?" I asked. "He has to be around somewhere."

Roy shook his head. "Clayton, Dixon, and Mike. Who's next?"

"You don't think he's dead, do you?" Good gravy! Metamora Mike, dead? I couldn't imagine. That duck was thought to be immortal. It sounds crazy, but what about this town wasn't crazy?

"Time will tell, Cameron Cripps-Hayman. Time will tell."

Roy was quiet, pointing me along the

route home in silence. It was so unlike him, I sensed he really, truly was shaken by the murders.

"You know," I said, "the cases we've solved all had a motive. These will, too. They weren't random." I hoped he'd realize that as long as there was no reason for someone to come after him, he'd be okay. We all would.

"Right here," he said, opening the door before I'd slowed down to a stop.

I slammed on the brakes in front of a dilapidated mobile home with stacked cinder blocks for steps to the door. The ice and snow hadn't covered the frozen mud that surrounded the base of the trailer. A crooked screen door banged in the wind.

It hit me that I didn't know a lot about Roy. His sarcasm and jibes worked like barbed wire, not letting anyone get too close. Did his alcoholism lead to this life, or was it the other way around? Did he have family?

Watching him sway and stumble into his house, I made a promise to myself to find out who Roy really was.

Johnna, Betty, and I headed east into Ohio the next morning, leaving Roy and Logan in the church basement to call the ice carvers about their picks. Anna hadn't shown up again and Logan wasn't talking about whatever had happened the night before. He looked even more downtrodden than when he'd left my house. I made Roy promise not to get him drunk. The last thing I needed was to be arrested for contributing to a minor's underage drinking.

I made Monica promise to check in with them. She said she would as long as I started looking for my own car, then she tossed me her keys. I didn't know what the big deal with me driving hers was anyway. She walked everywhere in town and if she was going somewhere else it was with Quinn and he drove them in his pickup.

"Are we almost there?" Johnna asked for the tenth time. "I have to tinkle."

"We have about twenty more minutes," I said. "Do you want me to stop at the next exit?"

"No, I can hold it."

It was an hour drive, but you would think we were going to the ends of the earth. Betty sat in the backseat clutching a tin filled with an assortment of cookies. Her shiny blue-black hair had dulled to an almost lavender color. Cass died it for her so Betty wouldn't have to spend the money to go to the beauty salon. Results varied.

"Betty, how long has it been since you last saw Lana?" I asked.

"Let's see, they were over for Old Dan's ninetieth birthday. Was that two years ago now or three?"

"More like five," Johnna said. "That was the year we were all at Ellsworth House on Christmas Eve since it was Old Dan's birthday. Irene and Stew still lived there. It was before Cameron moved here."

"That's right," Betty said. "I know I've seen Lana since then, though. That was such a long time ago. Oh, I know. It was Canal Days last year. She brought me a few loaves of bread made with wheat from their farm, and I gave her some strawberry shortbread cookies, Starnes's favorite."

"It's too bad she doesn't come to town more often," I said. Betty didn't drive, so I knew it was hard for her to travel to see anyone.

"She used to, but over the years it's not as easy to find the time, even for an hour drive."

"The farm must keep them busy," I said.

"Lana finds ways to keep herself busy," Johnna muttered.

"You don't believe that," Betty said, giving Johnna a playful swat on the shoulder. "I never knew of any proof, and she and I have always been close."

"What's this about?" I asked.

"Vicious rumors," Betty said. "People always liked to talk about Lana because she spent time at the Cornerstone without Starnes."

"She likes the men, that one does," Johnna said.

"Rumors!" Betty sat back in a huff.

"I guess that's as good of a reason as any to stay away then." If I were the subject of town gossip, I wouldn't come back for visits, either. "It was nice of you to bring the cookies," I said, bridging to another topic I had to get out of the way, and it was good that Johnna was in the car to hear it. "Speaking of baking, did Clayton Banks try to trade you a bunch of wheat flour for anything in the past week or so?"

"No," Betty said. "He knew better than to try to barter with me. I wasn't ever having any of it. Why?"

"Oh, no reason. We heard he was trying to wheel and deal with Carl Finch so I wondered if maybe he'd done the same with you."

"He knew I run a cash-only business. I don't bake on trade."

Johnna was true to her word and we didn't

93

have to stop until we got to Hamilton Wheat Farm and pulled up to the house. Acre after acre was covered in snow. You could see for miles in every direction. A few pine trees stood around the white farm house, two trucks and a car sat parked in the gravel driveway, and smoke rose from the chimney. We hadn't called first, and we were lucky that it looked as if they were home.

A dog raced up to the car, barking with her tail wagging. She was a big, tan mixed breed hound dog, and happy to see visitors.

"May Bell!" a trim woman with dusky blond hair who must be Lana called from the porch as we got out of the car. "May Bell, heel!"

The dog continued to trounce around us, bouncing and wagging, tongue lolling.

"Hello," Betty called, waving. "Hope it's okay that we stopped out to see you."

"Betty! What a surprise. And Johnna. Come on in." She turned her head to the side and called into the house. "Starnes! We have company!"

I wiped my feet on the mat and followed them inside. "This is Cameron Hayman," Betty said. "Irene and Stewart's daughter-in-law."

"I heard Ben got remarried," Lana said, shaking my hand. "It's nice to meet you,

Cameron."

"Nice to meet you, too."

She ushered us into the front room, which had a large open archway to the kitchen. A man, who I assumed was Starnes, waved and opened a door off the kitchen. "Good to see you. Compressor on the furnace is on the fritz. Just going down to do some work. You ladies have a nice chat." He slung a coil of copper tubing over his shoulder and tromped down the basement steps.

An enormous pot steamed on the kitchen stove, and Lana rushed in and turned it off. "Just making a big batch of corn bread," she said, and patted a big burlap bag of cornmeal with the Metamora Grist Mill's logo on it.

"Enough for an army, looks like," Johnna said, plopping down in a swivel chair beside the fireplace.

"It freezes well," Lana said. "Can I get you some coffee?"

"I brought cookies." Betty stepped toward the kitchen, but Lana rushed toward her taking them. "I hope those shortcake cookies are in here," she said, patting Betty's arm. "You know how much we love those."

"Of course! I made them special for you."

"I'll take some coffee," Johnna said.

"I'll help you get it," Betty offered, but

Lana shooed her back to the sofa.

"You sit and get comfortable. I'll be right there."

Lana wasn't a bad-looking woman, and I could see how in her younger years she would've turned the heads of men. That alone could earn a woman an unwarranted reputation.

I took a seat in a wooden rocking chair between the sofa and fireplace. On the mantel there were photos of families, parents posing with teenage kids. I figured it must be Lana and Starnes's kids and grandkids. Their kids might've gone to school with Jason Banks and Ben. "Did David Dixon ever have any kids?" I asked, wondering who stood to inherit.

"What's this about David Dixon?" Lana asked.

I realized my blunder instantly. Had word got around about Dixon's death?

"He's dead," Johnna said, not looking up from her knitting.

"Dead? What? How? But I thought Clayton . . . are both of them gone?" She sat on the sofa next to Betty, her face void of expression. The news hadn't hit her yet.

"It's terrible," Betty said. "Awful. He was killed last night at the winter festival."

"Killed? Both of them?" She shook her

head. "I don't understand how this is happening. Who would've . . ."

"We'll find out," I said. "I mean, my husband will find out. Ben."

"That's right. He's the sheriff in town now, isn't he?" Lana's brows lowered as she eyed me.

"He is. Yes."

A beep sounded from the kitchen. "That's the coffeemaker," Lana said. She rose from the sofa and padded across the carpet back into the kitchen.

"She's taking the news hard," Betty said.

"How could you tell?" I asked. "I couldn't read her expression."

"I know Lana. I can tell. She puts on a brave mask, but inside she's hurting. It's been a shock to us all."

"I'm sure it has." Ties ran deep in Metamora.

In the end, we only stayed a little over a half an hour. I didn't find Lana Buntley overly welcoming. Perhaps it was the shock of the sudden deaths of two long-time friends. Perhaps it was her desire to have an empty house when she broke the news to Starnes. Maybe it was a fear of her husband being next on the murderer's list considering his connection with the two victims.

Whatever the case, we were back on the

road in less time that it took to get there and Johnna was regretting downing a cup of coffee. "You're going to have to pull over this time, Cam," she said. I made a note to not let her have any beverages before or during our next car trip.

SIX

A family dinner Sunday night was just what the doctor ordered. We all needed some time to come together in the warmth and safety of Ellsworth House. I even invited Irene and Stew. Fortunately for everyone's stomaches, Monica agreed to cook.

Ben hovered while I set the table in the dining room that we never used outside of Thanksgiving and Christmas. "Why are you nervous?" I asked.

"I'm not nervous," he said, straightening the fork I just laid. "Why would I be nervous? I am curious, though."

"About?"

"This dinner. Do you have some announcement to make, Cam?"

"Announcement?" I placed the last silverware setting on the table and looked at him. "Oh . . ." I knew where this conversation was heading. Irene wanted us to either make up or break up, no more hemming and hawing around dating and seeing if we could get back together permanently.

Ben wanted to move back in. I'd told him I'd think about it. That was a few months ago now and I honestly had kept it in the back of my mind where it didn't get a whole lot of consideration.

I was for not messing with the status quo. It worked.

We had our movie nights. He stopped in whenever he felt like it. Mia lived here with me, he lived in Carl Finch's gate house, and all was right with the world.

"No," I said, taking a couple steps toward him. "I mean, that's not what I had in mind for tonight. I just thought it would be nice to get together after what happened last night — and the day before. I guess I felt like having family around."

He nodded and gave me a reluctant smile. "It's a nice idea. I like family dinners."

I knew what his words implied. He'd like a family dinner with me and Mia every night. It was like I was actually inside his mind sometimes. The trouble was when we did have family dinners every night, he worked through the majority of them. But that was in the past. We were trying things again. "We should do it more often," I said, meaning it. Our relationship was going well, so why not?

Ben reached out and rubbed my arm. "I'd like that."

"I would, too," I said, and he leaned down and kissed me lightly.

"What's this then?" Quinn asked, rushing in with a couple trivets and serving spoons. "Am I interrupting?"

"No," Ben said. "You're not interrupting. Does Monica have anything else she wants brought in? I'll go ask her."

He strode into the kitchen, and Quinn raised a brow in silent question.

"Nothing new to report," I told him.

"With this special dinner put on, I couldn't help wondering."

"Neither could he. If I knew that's what everyone would think I would've just put on my pj's and ordered a pizza."

"And miss out on Monica's pot roast and potatoes?"

"You're right. It's worth every question. It smells heavenly."

The doorbell rang right before I heard the front door open and Irene call, "Hello? We're here!" in her shrill, overly happy voice. Something told me she was expecting this to be the big announcement, too. The start of Ben and Cameron's reunion tour.

The dogs were barking, their nails tip-tapping on the hardwood as they scampered up the hallway. "Better go say hello," I said.

"I've got your back," Quinn said, chuckling as he followed me into the kitchen. As always, his dog, Conan, the dignified Irish Wolfhound, was sitting calmly, out of the way by the back door while my obnoxious pack jumped and licked and pawed at Irene and Stewart saying hello. Except Isobel, who stood in the living room growling because all she wanted in the world was to be left alone in her old age.

"Down!" I shouted. "Gus! Zack! Cody!"

"Zack and Cody?" Monica yelled from the kitchen. "What show is that from?"

The Suite Life of Zack and Cody," I called back. "It used to be on Saturday mornings."

"A kid's show, no doubt," Irene said. "I've never heard of it, and these beasts don't deserve such nice names." She picked up a magazine from the hall table where I dumped my mail, rolled it up, and waved it around in front of her, threatening the dogs.

"What happened to Nicky and Alex?" Monica asked, sweeping down the hallway to where we stood. She lured the dogs into the family room with her Bounding for Blueberry Dog Treats.

"It didn't stick." I'd never been the biggest *Full House* fan. I wasn't sure Zack and

102

Cody sounded right for my little brutes either, though.

Ben collected coats and everyone was seated in the dining room — including Mia, who came downstairs and even took out her earbuds and pocketed her phone.

"What a lovely table you've set," Irene said, studying the silver. "Was this my great-grandmother's serving spoon?" She picked up the antique and held it up toward the chandelier I was surprised was still attached to the ceiling and not hanging in her own dining room.

"Don't we have the matching meat fork at home?" Stewart asked, leaning in to examine the spoon.

"Yes, we do," she said, and tucked it into her purse. "You understand," she said, giving me a broad smile that could grace a poster at the dentist's office. "You can't break up the pair."

"Especially not family heirlooms," Stewart said, with a hearty laugh.

"I'll grab another spoon from the kitchen," Ben said shaking his head. He knew an antique serving piece wasn't worth putting up a fight over. He always told me that everything Irene took would find its way back to Ellsworth House in the end anyway. I supposed that was true enough.

"Need help in there, Monica?" I called. She'd already put rolls and vegetables on the table.

"No, I'm bringing the roast out now."

"I'll take this bowl of potatoes," I heard Ben say.

"I'll pour the wine," Quinn said, turning the corkscrew into the top of a bottle of Merlot.

Monica came to the doorway carrying a platter loaded with slices of steaming roast beef. It smelled so good, my mouth started watering. I couldn't wait to get my fork into — "No! Gus, move!" Monica shouted, lurching forward and tumbling over Gus.

The roast went flying. Monica landed on top of Gus, who let out a startled bark to match her shriek, and the platter landed with a thud, upside down on Stewart's foot.

"I just bought him those shoes!" Irene shouted. "Every time we come over here something gets ruined by those monsters of yours, Cameron!"

"My roast," Monica mumbled, watching the dogs chow down on the beef strewn across the carpet like it was the last food they'd ever get to eat.

Quinn helped her up and Ben got wet towels and carpet cleaning spray from the kitchen. Irene dabbed a napkin in her water glass and began scrubbing meat juice from Stewart's new shoe. Mia just shook her head and put her earbuds back in.

My eyes met Conan's, who was sitting in the corner of the room taking it all in, like he was wondering how he ended up in this circus.

I just wanted a nice family dinner, I tried to relay to him telepathically.

The road to Hell is paved with good intentions, he seemed to say back.

You're a wise dog, Conan. A wise, wise dog.

The next morning I woke to sun shining through my window and voices outside. I stretched, fought the dogs lying on top of my quilt to let me out of bed, and shuffled to the window. Down below on the bank of the canal, a group of people were searching the ice and snow. At first I thought they were going to go ahead with the hockey game, then Roy's words from the other night came rushing back.

They were searching for Metamora Mike.

Good gravy, had that duck really disappeared? I couldn't imagine the town without its feathered mascot waddling around the canal.

I dressed in a rush, and on my way downstairs banged on Monica and Mia's doors.

"We need to get outside!" I shouted. "Hurry!"

Monica threw her door open. "What's going on?" she asked, eyes wide and hair sticking out in all directions.

"Is the house on fire?" Mia yelled from her bedroom.

"No, Mike's missing!" I shouted. "The whole town is searching for him. We have to help!"

Monica groaned. "Give me five minutes."

Downstairs, I let the dogs out and made coffee. I was shocked when Mia found her way to the kitchen before Monica. She had boots on her feet, a hat on her head, and the dogs' leashes in her hands. "Steph says they've been looking since dawn and there's no sign of him," she said. "Do you think he flew south?"

"Roy says he never flies south."

"The canal never freezes over, either."

"That's true," I said, pouring a mug of coffee. "If we don't find him, I guess all we can do is wait until spring to see if he comes back."

I hooked the dogs up to their leashes, filled a travel mug with coffee for Monica, and met her at the bottom of the stairs. "Isobel doesn't want to go with us," she said, kneeling down and nuzzling the

106

grumpy German Shepherd. "She hates the cold. She has arthritis."

"And Liam's too little," Mia said, kissing her five-pound white ball of fur on the nose. "He'll stay here with Isobel."

In the end, Monica and Mia each took one of the twins, and I wrangled Gus out the door. "All right, Gus," I said, "find Mike."

To my surprise, Ben stood across the road on the bank with Brutus. He looked just as astonished to see us out. "I didn't think you'd get up so early to look for a duck," he said.

I shook my head. "It's not just any duck, Ben."

Admittedly, a year ago I would've never had anything to do with looking for a dumb duck that the town people — for reasons unknown — had taken as one of their own. But somehow I'd become integrated with these people and this place, and I felt invested in finding Mike as much as anyone else did.

I didn't miss the sly smile on Ben's face as he put an arm around Mia and kissed her on top of her head. "I was just about to take a team to the other end of the canal. Why don't you guys come with me?"

Gus and Brutus were busy sniffing and

jostling each other in greeting while the twins played at biting each other. "The twins are questionable, but I think these two can find him," I said. "Let's get going."

The dogs sniffed the wet, slushy ground being thawed by the rising temperature and shining sun. Soapy and Theresa waved from the opposite side of the canal. I spotted Johnna riding her power scooter across the bridge. We caught up with her on the other side.

"Where are you headed?" I asked.

She patted a few items in the basket on front of her scooter, tucking the ends of a grocery bag closed around a loaf of bread. "Just taking a couple things over to Roy. That drunkard can't take care of himself." She snorted in derision, pursing her lips.

"That's nice of you," I said.

Who was I kidding? Nice or not, it was the very last thing I expected from Johnna. She and Roy were constantly at each other's throats. But I found myself at a lack for words.

"Better get going," she said, buzzing her scooter around us. "Gotta get back home to my Charlie." One of the twin terriers nipped at her back tire and barked as she rode off. He pulled at his leash, urging Monica to follow Johnna.

"We're not going that way," Monica said, tugging back.

We trotted on, scouring the bank, the gazebo, and around the tree growing sideways along the ground. It was an enormous tree that had bent over sideways and continued to grow, making yet another oddity for Metamora. A grounded, horizontal tree. The kids loved to play on it, and it was a nice spot for seniors to sit in the shade.

I felt someone watching me, and turned to look behind me. In the distance, Jason Banks stood with Ginger, the Chow Chow. Her blue tongue lolled out of her mouth as she stood panting with her breath turning white in the air. As soon as we made eye contact, he glanced away.

"I think he and I need to have words," Ben said, watching.

"It's fine," I said, shaking off the eerie feeling. "He's grieving and misplacing his anger."

"Exactly, and he's not going to get away with making my wife feel threatened."

Before I could respond, he stormed off toward the bridge to confront Jason. I couldn't help but wonder what their relationship was like in high school. Ben seemed to have no love for Jason, and I was sure the feeling was mutual.

"That duck is gone," Monica said, leading the twin formerly known as Cody toward me.

Mia was busy texting on her phone. "Can I go to the Soda Pop Shop to meet Steph?" she asked.

"Go ahead." I took the other twin terrier from her, holding my arms wide to keep him and Gus from tangling their leads.

"How do you feel about getting a muffin or something from Soapy Savant?" Monica asked. "My stomach's growling."

"We might as well. Let's drop the dogs off at home."

As we headed back toward Ellsworth House, the terrier she was walking pulled on his leash, wanting to turn down the road where Johnna had gone toward Roy's. He parked it and tugged, digging his back feet into the frozen ground.

"Stop!" Monica shouted, pulling him back with all of her might. "He's so strong," she said. "Give me a hand."

Already having two dogs, I was hardly able to help her. "Heel!" I yelled. "Hey — you — this way!"

"You need to name these dogs!" Monica said, slipping and sliding, trying to get the dog back on the right path home. "They don't respond to *hey you.*"

A sharp whistle sounded close to us, distracting the dogs. We all turned to see Quinn coming our direction. "Thank the heavens, the dog trainer's here," Monica said.

"We need to get these boys behaved," he said, taking the leash from Monica. In two seconds he had the dog back by his side and sitting.

"I don't know how you do it," I said.

"He's the alpha," Monica gushed, grinning like a girl with her first crush.

"I've always had a way with animals," Quinn said.

"We were on our way to the Soapy Savant after we take the dogs home if you'd like to join us," I said.

"Absolutely. I could do with a cup of hot tea. No luck with the duck hunt?"

"No."

"He'll show up. I'm sure he's lived through winters this cold before."

"Everyone's been leaving stale bread out for him in case he's around," Monica said.

"I'd not be lured back by stale bread, would you?" Quinn asked. "Maybe you should put out some of your dog treats. They're grain based, but have a good flavor. He might be tempted to show up for one."

"That's a good idea," she said. "I think

the new blueberry ones might be good."

"Do ducks like blueberries?" I wondered out loud.

"That duck probably likes most human food," Quinn said. "He's more domestic duck than wild."

"True." I shrugged. We'd see if Mike liked dog treats enough to show himself if he really was around.

We let the dogs inside, Monica grabbed some treats, and we trudged through the slush and ice across the bridge. At the edge of the canal, Monica tossed her treats along the bank, scattering them around in various spots. Then we made our way to the Soapy Savant.

The coffee shop was packed. Most of the members of the search party had ended up inside getting warm with a hot beverage. We found a table along the back wall and sat down.

"Okay, dog names," Monica said. "We're not leaving here until you decide on something."

"Right now?" I'd been so indecisive about names for the two twin dogs, I couldn't even fathom picking something and sticking with it.

"Right now," Monica said, and Quinn nodded in agreement.

"You can't begin to train them until they know their names," he said. "They need individual identities."

"I've been trying to think of names," I said. "Twins from TV and movies. Nicky and Alex, Zack and Cody, Fred and George . . ."

"We'll help." Monica began to list famous duos. "Abbott and Costello? Archie and Jughead? Cheech and Chong?"

"Bo and Luke?" Quinn asked, getting in on the act.

"How do you know early-eighties American TV?" Monica asked him.

"Sometimes I can't sleep and watch late-night TV."

"Bo and Luke . . ." I pondered. "I don't think that's it. Definitely not Abbott and Costello."

"Bert and Ernie!" Monica said.

"What are we talking about?" Soapy asked, coming up to the table. *"Sesame Street?"*

"We're trying to name my dogs," I told him.

"About time. What can I get you folks?"

We ordered and Soapy chimed in with his own suggestion. "Kirk and Spock."

"Nothing sounds like them. They have their own personalities. Maybe that's the problem. They don't act like Kirk and Spock or Ernie and Bert."

"Jekyll and Hyde," Soapy offered, with a snicker. "I'll get your drinks."

At the next table over, Old Dan and his son Frank had overheard our discussion and offered a few suggestions. "Fred and Barney," Frank said.

"Laurel and Hardy," Old Dan suggested.

"My mind is on overload," I said. "So many names."

"Just pick one. Well, two," Monica said. "It's not that hard."

"It is hard. I don't want to stick them with names that don't fit them. The problem is they're unique. They need their own names, so all these famous pairs just won't work."

"We're not leaving until you name them," Monica repeated.

"Good gravy, we'll be here all day."

Monica sighed. "We can't be here all day. I have dog treats to make. My Colby Jack Puppy Snacks are running low."

"Colby Jack," I said, letting the name of a tasty cheese mull in my brain. "Colby and Jack." A zing of knowing shot through me. "That's it! Those are the names. Colby and Jack!"

"You're naming your dogs after cheese?" Quinn asked.

"I guess I am." I couldn't stop smiling. The names seemed to be perfect. "Colby and Jack, leaders of the pack."

"Isobel might have something to say about that," Monica said, laughing.

"And Gus," Quinn added.

"Goofballs of the pack maybe," I said. "But still, those are their names. I'm going to go home and tell them the news."

"I'll double my batch of Colby Jack treats so they can have some to celebrate."

"I'll help," I said.

We got our drinks to go so we could get back to Ellsworth House and start baking. On our way out the door Ben and Sheriff Reins were coming in. Reins was holding his handcuffs.

"What's going on?" I asked.

"Go home, Cam," Ben said. "We're making an arrest."

"What? Who? Why?"

Without answering he brushed by me and the two officers headed directly for the table where Old Dan and Frank Gardner sat.

"Dan Gardner," Sheriff Reins said, "Frank Gardner, you're under arrest for the murder of Clayton Banks."

My mouth dropped open and I could barely hear Reins read them their rights over the buzzing in my brain. This couldn't be.

Old Dan and his son wouldn't murder anyone.

SEVEN

Logan practically burst with cockiness. "I told you the wheat was probably poisoned," he said. "Those told timers ground up that wheat and poisoned Clayton Banks with it."

"They did no such thing," Johnna said, slapping the tabletop and making Colby bark. "They're innocent as the day is long."

The Action Agency had all found their way to my house as soon as the word got out about the arrests.

"Ben said the autopsy shows poisoning by *Lolium temulentum*." Logan spun his laptop around to show us the screen. "Poison darnel is the common name. It looks like wheat and used to get mixed in with wheat and accidentally poisoned people until modern machinery was invented that sifts it out."

"That still doesn't mean that Old Dan and Frank are responsible," I said. "And the autopsy wasn't conclusive."

"Conclusive enough to make an arrest," Logan said.

"So you think Old Dan offed him then?" Roy asked Logan. "Easy as that? Case closed? You hardly even know him or his son, and what does any of this have to do with Dixon? You want to tell me it was a coincidence that he took an ice pick to the head?"

"I'm just going by the facts," Logan said.

Roy and Logan had contacted all the contestants at the ice sculpting contest and they all were in possession of their tools. None had gone missing.

"Facts ain't nothing without context," Roy said. He'd been in a somber mood ever since finding out about the arrest this morning. "If Old Dan killed that man, I'll never drink another drop."

"That's committing to your beliefs," Quinn said from behind the kitchen counter where he and Monica were finishing up the last batch of Colby Jack Puppy Snacks.

"I hope Ben can find out if any more of that wheat was consumed," Monica said.

"He's gone to talk to Jason Banks to see if there's any in the house, or if he knows where his dad would've gotten it." I couldn't stop pacing the kitchen. "It's obviously from Starnes."

"So why wasn't Starnes arrested?" Johnna asked.

"Maybe he will be," I said. "We don't know."

"They can't keep them locked up," Roy said. "There ain't enough evidence that they done anything wrong."

"They took money for a service and provided a tainted product," I said. "If that product led to Clayton's death, they'll be held responsible. Starnes will too if it comes out that he provided that wheat mixed with the darnel."

"It ain't right," Roy said, shaking his head.

Johnna reached across the table and patted his hand. "You know as well as I do they won't hold them long. Just think back to John Bridgemaker and Paul Foxtracker during the last murder investigation in this town. They even locked up Andy for a while."

"Old Dan don't belong in there."

"Wait," Monica said, holding up a finger. "Listen. What is that?"

We all fell silent. There was a faint keening coming from outside, like an injured bird.

"On my life!" Johnna said, scrambling to her feet. "I think that's Mike!"

We all ran for the front door only to open

119

it to Elaina Nelson wailing on my front porch.

"Mrs. Nelson," I said, "what in the world are you doing out here in the freezing cold all alone? Come inside!" I would not be held responsible for a ninety-something-year-old woman coming down with pneumonia from camping out crying on my porch.

"Dan killed a man," she sobbed, while I hauled her inside and Johnna tucked a throw from the back of my couch around her shoulders.

"Now, he did no such thing, dear," Johnna said, leading her into the kitchen. "Cameron, make her some tea."

I did what I was told, and also sent a text to Mia asking her to tell Steph where her great-grandma was. Odds were good that Elaina's family was looking for her.

Elaina sniveled and sipped her tea, and I felt so terrible that Ben had anything to do with arresting Old Dan that I wanted to crawl under the table and hide. How could he do it? He had to know Dan and Frank would never do such a thing.

I could hear Ben now. *It's my job, Cameron. What did you expect me to do? Break the law and not arrest them?*

It was just one more example of how his job as a cop came between us. Of course I wanted him to do the right thing, but in this case I couldn't see how arresting the oldest person in town was the right thing.

"He won't survive in a cell," Elaina said. "He'll catch his death in there."

"Cameron Cripps-Hayman," Roy said, and I knew I was in for it with him calling me by my full name, "why can't your husband put one of them ankle bracelet thingies on him and let him go home?"

"He won't go nowhere," Elaina said, wiping her tears, her brows arched with hope.

"Well, I don't know. Why don't I call and find out?" At least it would get me out of the room and away from the accusing stares.

I disappeared into the dining room and dialed Ben's number, fuming more and more with every ring of his cell phone. "Cam, I don't have time to talk right now. Why don't I call you —"

"You listen to me, Benjamin Hayman. I have a crying Elaina Nelson in my kitchen along with a cantankerous Roy. It's taking all I have not to find you and demand answers, so you're lucky all you're getting is a phone call."

He let out a long, heavy sigh, and I could picture that look on his face, the one he reserved just for me, the mixture of frustration, annoyance, and irritation. "I told you

121

everything I know, now let me get back to work."

"Do you actually think that old man poisoned Clayton Banks?"

"No. Of course I don't. But that's where the flour came from that poisoned him, so we have enough evidence to arrest and hold them. If they aren't guilty, they'll be released."

"Can't you slap an ankle bracelet on him and let him go home? Prison is no place for a man who's nearing a century old."

"He has every comfort, Cam. We're keeping them in the gate house at Carl's place."

"You're . . . where will you stay then?"

"I was hoping I could come home."

"Oh. Well, of course." I supposed this settled things. He was coming back home. "I'll see you later then."

"Cam, I can stay at the Fiddle Dee Doo."

"No, there's no reason for that." This was his house, after all. If I hadn't determined that I wanted to stay apart after almost a year, then it was time to try to be together full-time again. This was just the push my procrastination needed.

"Okay then," he said. "I'll be home in time for dinner with you and Mia."

"And Monica and Quinn if they're here," I added.

"And the pack of dogs we've accumulated."

"And them," I said, chuckling.

"It's really become a madhouse over there," he said, and I heard the laughter in his voice.

"You don't have to tell me. I haven't even mentioned Johnna and Logan. Oh, and there's a knock at the door."

"It's probably Andy. You better go answer it. I'll be home soon."

He'd be home soon.

I said goodbye and hung up feeling happy, but afraid. This was the plunge off of the high dive I'd been avoiding. I didn't know why exactly until now, but it hit me that this was our last chance. If it didn't work this time, it never would. I couldn't put it off any longer.

As I stepped back into the kitchen, Andy and Monica were coming in from the hallway. "I just heard," he said. "There's no way in —"

"I know," I said. "But I just talked to Ben. Old Dan and Frank aren't being kept in jail." I explained what I knew about the men being held at the gate house. "So they're officially being held, but not behind bars."

"Well, at least that's something," Roy said, patting Elaina gently on the shoulder. "Want a nip in your tea to calm the nerves?" He held out his flask and Elaina nodded, giving him a watery smile.

He poured in a generous amount, almost overflowing her cup. I noticed her right hand was in her lap stroking a black cat. Spook, the cat who showed up and sneaked in somehow, was back. I'd found him inside Carl Finch's Hilltop Castle once, so I knew he prowled around breaking and entering into people's homes all over town. The dogs never even seemed to notice him, which was why I took to calling him Spook. He was rather ghostlike, appearing and disappearing at will.

There was another knock on the door. "Come in!" Monica shouted. "What?" she asked me. "I'm tired of answering it. You might as well leave it wide open."

The door opened and closed, and light footsteps sounded descending the hallway. Then Anna appeared, looking shy and defeated. "I can't believe this," she said. "I came right when I heard."

"Good to have you back," I said, putting an arm around her shoulder and leading her to the table. "We need the full brain power of the Action Agency to figure this out."

"Don't forget us honorary members,"

Quinn said.

"We need all the brain cells we can get," I told him, nodding to Monica and Andy as well.

"Here's to brain cells," Roy said, holding up his flask and taking a deep drink.

Good gravy. Maybe AA shouldn't stand for Action Agency in Roy's case.

Monica had ushered all of my emotional guests out of the house before Ben got home, then she and Quinn made themselves scarce, going to his house in Connersville for dinner. "I have to check in at the kennel," Quinn had said. "I'll keep your sister out of your house tonight."

"It's okay," I told him. "It's not like she's a pesky little nine-year-old."

"Either way, it would be my privilege." He winked.

Mia texted telling me school was just canceled for the following day and asking to spend the night at Steph's. She didn't know Ben was coming home to stay and I was sure he'd want to tell her. ASK YOUR DAD, I texted back, feeling like I was channeling my own mother when I wrote it. A few minutes later she sent me another saying that her dad told her it was okay to stay overnight with Steph.

So it would be just Ben and me. Would he have expectations of a romantic reunion? I wandered around the house. The dogs were curled up in the family room sleeping after gorging on freshly baked treats. With everyone gone I could hear the wind blowing against the house, making the walls creak. The cold air coming in from the north was turning all of the day's melting slush to ice.

I thought about my bees in their hive, clustered together, shivering, wings fluttering, desperate to keep their queen warm. I hadn't told them about Old Dan, the man who built their bee box and moved them from my porch column. The man who would sit in a lawn chair beside their hive and sing to them. He warned me if I didn't keep them up to date on the town gossip, they'd swarm.

I knew they were bees. I knew it was folklore, but I also felt responsibility to Old Dan. He'd want them to know.

I bundled up and headed out my front door. The world was made of crystal that shined and shimmered in my porch lights. My boots crunched through the icy snow on the steps. I'd have to ask Andy — no, I didn't need Andy's help anymore. Ben could shovel the steps.

I'd become so used to Andy hanging

around all the time, what would I do without him? What would he do without a job being my handyman?

I made my way over to the bee box in the yard between the sidewalk and flowerbed. Somehow I'd escaped being fined by the Daughters of Metamora for having it in my front yard. I was certain they found it unsightly, but I didn't want the dogs anywhere near it — for their safety and that of the bees — so it wasn't going in my backyard.

"Hello," I said, leaning toward the top. "It's me, Cameron. I have some bad news to tell you. Old Dan was arrested today. Don't worry, he didn't actually do anything, I'm sure of that. He'll be released soon. You probably heard all the chatter out here this morning," I said, leaning against their wooden home, getting comfortable. "Metamora Mike is missing."

I stood there filling them in on everything from the murders to Ben coming home. I found that once I started talking to the bees, I couldn't stop. Knowing that they were in there listening, but not offering advice and not judging, had cut my tongue loose. I was so engaged in talking, I didn't hear Ben pull in the driveway and walk up behind me.

"Are you talking to the bees?" he asked.

I jumped, startled, slid on the icy sidewalk, and flailed, circling my arms like wings trying to save myself from going down. Ben grasped my hand, and Brutus attempted to break my fall, but it wasn't enough. I fell like a ton of bricks and felt a spike of white hot pain shoot through my wrist.

"I have to be honest Cam, I didn't picture us spending tonight in the emergency room." Ben smiled, brushing my hair back from my forehead.

"Expect the unexpected," I said.

"Oh, I do. I married you, after all."

Ben's cell phone buzzed. He had his ringer on silent, but he answered. "I'll be right there," he said.

He hung up and said, "That was the coroner. The toxicology report for Clayton is finally finished, so we'll know if it was a fatal amount of the poisoned darnel that killed him."

"And if it wasn't a fatal amount, then it wasn't the darnel?"

"Yeah, and we can release Old Dan and Frank." He stood and headed for the door. "I'll be back soon."

"Go," I said, anxious to know the fate of my favorite old timer.

Ben left and the doctor bustled in with a

laptop. "It's broken," he said. "Let me show you the X-ray." He showed me the black-and-white photos of my arm and said something about it being a common fracture and nothing to be worried about. He didn't want to cast it due to the swelling, so it would be wrapped tight and put in a sling. I'd have to come back in a few days to get a cast.

After what seemed like forever, my arm was wrapped up like a mummy and I was given a prescription for pain pills and sent on my way. I texted Ben to tell him I was in the waiting room and released to my destiny. He texted back that he'd get the truck and to watch for him out the windows.

Ben pulled Metamora One around to the ER exit door and helped me up into the cab. "I suppose we should find a pharmacy that's open and get some fast food, too," he said.

It was almost ten at night. We'd spent just under five hours at the hospital. Having a past career in a call center environment, I couldn't help but think in terms of efficiency and productivity. It was always my opinion that hospitals could use a dose of productivity training.

I yawned and nodded. "I could go for a cheeseburger. Oh, that reminds me. I named the twin terrier tanks." I told him about Colby and Jack.

"I like those names, they're good, solid names."

He shut my door and rounded the front of the truck, getting in the driver's side and heading out of the hospital parking lot.

My mind was hazy from the pain medication the doctor had given me, so it took me a couple minutes to remember what was nagging at me. "Clayton," I finally said. "What did the report say?"

"It was inconclusive," he said. "He had a toxic amount of the darnel in his system, but not a fatal amount. He died of cardiac arrest. The coroner isn't convinced that the darnel attributed to the cardiac arrest, and therefore, his murder. He also had other drugs in his system — medication, whether prescribed or not. That has to be determined as well."

"What other drugs?" I asked.

"Blood pressure medication," he said.

"Blood pressure medication shouldn't kill him though, should it?"

"Not normally, and they weren't toxic or fatal doses, either. I need to talk to his doctor and find out what he was on and for how long."

"So are you releasing Old Dan and

Frank?"

"That's for Sheriff Reins to decide. It was his arrest warrant."

"That doesn't make me feel all warm and fuzzy, Ben."

"No, and it shouldn't."

"What about Starnes Buntley? It was his wheat. How did Clayton end up eating some?"

"Starnes is being held in Hamilton, Ohio. If the wheat flour killed Clayton, he's just as responsible as Old Dan and Frank."

"So what now? If there wasn't fatal levels of any of the drugs in his system, how do you know he didn't just have a heart attack and die?"

"The drugs have to be ruled out as the cause. If it was a natural death, the investigation ends and all charges are dropped, of course."

"But what about Dixon? *That* wasn't natural. Don't you think the same person killed both men?"

"At present, we have no evidence of that. The causes of death are completely different."

"But they were close friends. That can't be coincidental."

"They're being treated as separate investigations," he said, and that was his final word on the Dixon case.

The Action Agency had our work cut out for us. The list was a big one. We'd have to, A) prove Clayton was murdered, 2) prove that both murders were committed by the same person, and thirdly, find the killer.

Who was I kidding? It would take nothing short of a miracle this time around.

EIGHT

There was no avoiding it. I had to tell a fib. Well, it was an omission, really. "I'm going to the grocery store," I told Ben, who was outside getting ready to snow blow and salt the sidewalk. After my fall the evening before, he'd spent the morning buying all of the snow-removal products one man could ever hope to own.

"You can't shop with your arm in a sling. I'll go after I clear the driveway," he said.

I couldn't think of a way around that one, so I smiled and went back inside. "Darn," I said after closing the door.

"What's the matter?" Monica asked, heading toward the washing machine with a clothes basket.

"I need to talk to Jason Banks, but I can't let Ben know. He'd never let me question him after Jason threatened me."

"Speaking of which, the scabs on your face are almost gone."

"That's the least of my problems," I said, "but thanks."

"Can't you just call him?" Monica opened the closet door that the washer sat behind and started tossing clothes inside.

"I need to see his face to know if he's telling me the truth. And I want to snoop around the house. I need a way over there."

"Why don't we say we're going somewhere and we'll stop by Clayton's house?"

"I can't ask you to lie to Ben for me."

She dumped some detergent into the washer and pushed the buttons to get it started. "It's not lying if we go where we tell him we're headed. We'll just make a pit stop on the way."

This snooping thing was going to be a lot harder with Ben back home.

I went back to the front door and called out to Ben, letting him know that Monica was taking me to the grocery because she needed a few things, too.

"I might like this sister-in-law living with us situation," he said, giving me a wink. "Be careful."

We packed ourselves into Monica's little car and buzzed out to the main road. "Where to?" she asked.

I gave her directions and sat there feeling awful. My arm throbbed and guilt was eating me alive. "Maybe we shouldn't do this."

"Would you do it if Ben hadn't moved back home?"

"Of course, because I wouldn't have to sneak to do it!"

"You need to be honest with him, give up solving these murders, or get used to fudging the truth. It's your decision."

"I know, but it's not that easy."

"We'll get you through this, find the killer, and then it's over. No more playing crime solver and no more lying."

I took a deep breath, nodding. "Okay. You're right. It's not like this will be the situation forever, just until this is figured out."

Feeling a little better, I came up with a plan to get inside Clayton's house. "Do you have any dog treats with you?"

"Of course I do. Boxes full in the back." Monica pointed over her shoulder with her thumb. "Are you planning to bribe Jason with tasty treats?"

"Something like that."

I dug through my handbag. I had to have a ribbon or twine, something I could tie into a bow to make one of the boxes look like a peace offering present. My pain pills rattled around inside, and all I could come up with was some unraveled yarn that Johnna had given me to use as a bookmark. It wouldn't be long enough to tie into a bow even if I'd wanted to use it.

"What do you need?" Monica asked, pulling her purse up from the floor by my feet.

"Something to make into a bow."

"I should have a ribbon in there. It was tied around a bunch of flowers that Quinn brought to Dog Diggity last week."

"Flowers, what a gentleman."

Ben used to bring me flowers when we were first dating, too. The romance wore off around the time I started washing his socks.

I found the magenta ribbon in Monica's bag and wrapped it around my hand, fidgeting. "I hope this works. He's not exactly friendly."

"I'll be there this time. He won't try doing anything to you."

"I don't think he would, but I need to get inside."

"What are you snooping for?" she asked, glancing over at me.

"Pills, mainly. Blood pressure pills." I told her what the toxicology report said. "So you see why I have to get inside."

"I'll help."

When we pulled in the driveway I noted Jason's car was there along with a couple others. "Hurry and help me get the dog treats tied with this ribbon," I said, darting around to the back of her car.

Monica opened the hatchback and grabbed a box of treats. "They aren't even in the Dog Diggity packaging yet."

"This is no time to be picky about it." I watched her tie the ribbon around the box and slam the hatchback closed. "Let's do this."

"You look like a duck with a wounded wing in that puffy coat with your arm in a sling." She snickered behind me. "I found Mike!"

"Watch the slippery sidewalk and those Barberry bushes, or you won't be laughing any longer." I should know since I'd become a pro at falling on icy sidewalks.

We stepped up onto the cement slab porch and I rang the doorbell. I heard Ginger barking, and heeled shoes coming toward the door. A second later, the knob turned and a woman I'd never seen before stood in the doorway.

"Come in," she said. "It was nice of you to come. Are you a neighbor of Clayton's? I'm his sister-in-law, Robin."

She shook our hands. "Yes, we're from town," I said, a little bewildered at being let inside so easily.

"Let me take your coats," she said. "We

have refreshments in the dining room. Jason said he was keeping the burial private. I'm glad to see he invited someone to the wake."

Good gravy, a wake? Was Clayton's body here? On display? Was this the viewing for family? "Actually," I said, "we didn't know. We only stopped by to see how Jason was getting along."

"Oh, I see," she said. "Well, come in anyway and have a seat. I'll get him." She led us to the living room where an urn stood on a coffee table in the middle of the room surrounded by flowers. Ginger stood beside it as if she was on guard duty.

"Thank the Lord," Monica whispered behind me.

I couldn't agree more. I didn't want to see Clayton Banks laid out in his finest when I wasn't invited to do so. At least this was a little less intrusive.

"What are you doing here?" Jason asked, sweeping into the room. Ginger barked and let out a low growl, hearing his agitation.

"Jason," his aunt said, taking a hold of his arm, "these are your father's neighbors."

"They're nobody," he said. "And they're leaving."

"We brought a gift for Ginger," Monica said, taking the box from me and holding it out to Jason. He hesitated to take it at first, but finally grabbed it. "We have six dogs in our house and know how hard it must be for her to not have Clayton around. If you need help finding her a home, please let us know. We've placed several dogs with new owners."

Jason's expression went from anger to confusion to acceptance. He nodded but didn't say anything.

"Who's this then?" a man asked, breezing into the room carrying the strong scent of alcohol with him. He wore a gray suit and what I was certain was a hairpiece on his head.

"Dear," Robin said, "these are Clayton's neighbors." She turned to us. "I'm sorry, I didn't get your names."

"Cameron," I said, "and this is Monica, my sister."

"Nice to meet you," Monica said.

"Richard," the man said, shaking our hands. "Clayton's brother."

"We're sorry for your loss," I said.

"Thank you," he said, but waved the sentiment away. "Unfortunately, we hadn't spent much time together over the past few years. Decades, really."

"I'm sorry to hear that," I said, not sure how to respond to that statement.

"Funny thing," Richard continued, "we'd

had this trip planned for a few weeks now. I figured it was time to bury the hatchet with my brother. We were both getting on in years. I didn't want to lose the chance to make things right with him."

It was the saddest thing I'd ever heard. "That's . . ." I shook my head. "I can't imagine. I'm very sorry this happened."

"Please," Robin said, gesturing toward the sofa, "have a seat." Her pale face was blotched with red. I had a feeling her husband had a lot to say after he got some drinks down.

"Would it be too much trouble if I used your bathroom?" Monica asked, lowering her head, like she was embarrassed to ask.

"Of course not," Richard said. "Right down this hall here. Second door on your right."

"Thank you."

Jason watched her walk down the hallway, glowering after her. I had to talk to him and find out if his hostility toward us was all because of Ben and the skiing event I went ahead with, or if there was something more to it. I'd never get answers out of him about his dad's death unless I got past this barrier between us.

I sat down and tried to not look awkward and uncomfortable, but sitting there with the three of them watching me expectantly was a little off-putting.

"Was the service today?" I asked, eyeing the urn. "Those are beautiful flowers."

"We had the reverend from the church in town say a prayer at the funeral home. It was just us," Robin said.

"Dad didn't believe in church," Jason said.

"Well, we do," Richard said, putting a large hand on Jason's shoulder, almost like he was trying to keep his thirty-something nephew in line. "How did you know my brother, Cameron?"

I steered clear of festival talk and explained about how I'd first met Clayton in town trying to trade an arrowhead he'd found on his property for a new tractor seat.

"That was my brother!" Richard exclaimed, and laughed. "Always wheeling and dealing!"

"Yes, he was," I said, laughing along with him. "Did you grow up in Metamora as well?"

"I did, yes," Richard said. "I'm a handful of years older than Clayton. When I went away to college I ended up getting a job in Kentucky after graduation and that was that. Robin and I got married and we've lived near Lexington for too many years to count now."

"Did you go to high school with Soapy?" I asked. "Oh, I guess he wouldn't have been called that back then."

"I know he's called Soapy these days," Richard said, grinning. "I did go to school with him. I'm not surprised he became mayor. He was always the most popular kid in school."

I kept trying to make small talk while Monica searched the bathroom.

"Jason, will you be staying in town now? Living here?" I asked.

"Haven't decided yet," he said, not even looking at me as he replied. It was as if he was disgusted by my presence. I'd never experienced anything like it before. People liked me. This guy was making me feel self-conscious.

I wanted to bring up David Dixon, ask what they thought about Clayton's buddy being killed one day after he was. But I didn't want to rile up Jason by prying into his father's business. If only I could get him alone and tell him the Action Agency was trying to help find out what happened to his father. Maybe he wouldn't hate me then.

"Can I get you some coffee, or tea maybe?" Robin asked. "It's cold out there today."

"Please, don't go to any trouble. I'm fine,

142

thank you."

There was a knock at the front door. We all turned to look at it. "Well," Robin said, "this is nice. More visitors!"

She strode across the carpet toward the front door and swung it open. Lana Buntley stood on the porch. "Lana," Richard said, his mouth open and eyes going wide for a split second. "Hello." He plastered a smile on his face and went to stand with his wife, welcoming their new, unexpected guest.

Jason strode away, disappearing through the dining room into what I assumed was the kitchen. He came back a moment later with a beer in his hand. He plopped down in the armchair beside the sofa and took a deep drink, eyeing his father's urn. Ginger padded over and put her head on his knee.

"She likes you," I said.

He nodded, stroking her fur. "Why are you really here?"

"I'm trying to find out what happened to your dad. Ben doesn't know I'm here."

"Is that why your sister is poking around in the bathroom drawers?"

"What? Is she?" I blinked, innocently.

Jason shook his head. "You have a terrible poker face."

Lana came in the room with Richard and Robin. She took a seat beside me on the sofa. "Cameron, it's nice to see you again."

"You too," I said. "How's Starnes holding up?"

She looked down at her hands in her lap. "This has been such a terrible weekend. Filled with tragedy."

"I'm sorry for your loss, and please pass along my condolences to Starnes."

"Thank you."

Her hands shook like leaves, and I noticed a quiver in her head as well. It made me wonder if it was something more than grief that was affecting her.

Monica came down the hall and hesitated for a second at seeing another woman in the room. "Hello," she said, finally striding forward with a smile on her face.

"Monica," I said, "this is Lana Buntley, I don't believe you've met before."

"No, we haven't." Monica shook Lana's shaky hand. "Nice to meet you."

"You, too," Lana said, not making eye contact with Monica, or anyone in the room.

"Well," I said, starting to get up to make our departure just as another knock sounded at the door.

"This is exactly what I didn't want," Jason said, bolting out of his chair. "It's like Grand Central now."

Ginger began barking and followed him to the door. Jason yanked it open and sneered. "Come to get your wife?"

Ben stood in the doorway. He glanced my way, but the stern expression on his face didn't flicker. "I have a warrant to search the premises," he said.

"Search the premises? For what? My father was murdered, you moron!"

"Please, Officer," Richard said, rushing to Jason's side. "We're having a wake for my brother. Can't this wait?"

"I'm sorry for the timing," Ben said. "I won't disturb your guests. What I need won't take long to find. If you could lead me to Clayton's medications and any alcohol he has in the house — specifically moonshine — then I'll be on my way."

"Yes, yes, of course," Richard said. "Jason, sit down, son. I'll help the officer. You relax."

"Relax when the cops are searching the house," Jason scoffed, glaring at Ben. "I'll get you what you need. You're not welcome inside."

"This warrant says otherwise," Ben said.

Monica elbowed me, and covertly shoved a pill bottle into my hand. "Shove it in the cushions," she whispered.

I got her drift. We didn't need to be in possession of criminal evidence, if that's what these pills ended up being.

I stretched and turned my body a little, away from the door where Ben stood. Beside me, Lana was fussing with her handbag that sat on the floor.

I shoved the pill bottle between the couch cushions, and Lana shoved a mason jar full of clear liquid farther down inside her bag.

Good gravy, I'd just hidden the pills Ben was after, and did Lana just hide the moonshine?

NINE

It had been two hours since I'd gotten home from Clayton's house. Monica and I bolted as soon as Ben got inside and started his search in the kitchen. He hadn't even glanced our direction.

I paced from room to room, picking up clutter, dusting, and munching at least half a dozen of Betty's Apple Pie cookies with white chocolate chips. White chocolate wasn't my favorite, but I wouldn't refuse it in desperate times.

And I was desperate.

Who was I kidding? I was on the verge of being charged with tampering with evidence by my own husband. I was more than desperate.

Monica had escaped to Dog Diggity. Mia was still with Steph, and I was left to deal with Ben on my own when he came home.

What if he didn't find the pill bottle I hid in the couch cushions? It didn't seem like he was planning on tearing the house apart, especially not during Clayton's wake. And what about Lana's moonshine?

I had to tell him where to look. But I really, really, really didn't want that information coming from me. There was only one thing to do.

I grabbed my cell phone and dialed Andy's number. "I need a huge favor," I said when he answered.

"I take it it's not snow removal," he said. "Were you going to tell me I'm fired?"

My stomach sank. "I'm so sorry. Ben came back home last night. The situation happened kind of suddenly. The gate house is being used to hold Old Dan and Frank. I meant to call you."

"But you didn't need a favor until now."

"Andy, please don't be mad. I'm truly sorry. My mind has been all over the place."

He sighed. "I knew Ben would move back eventually. I should've been looking for something permanent all along."

"You weren't planning on staying in Metamora."

"I know. I don't know what I'm doing now. My documentary isn't finished. There's Cass . . ." he trailed off.

"It's just a suggestion," I said, hit with a brainstorm, "but nobody's running the mill while Old Dan and Frank are under lock and key at the gate house. Maybe you could pay them a visit and see what needs to be done?"

"I could do that," he said, sounding encouraged. "That would buy me some time to figure out what I'm going to do next."

"We take care of each other here," I told him. "You'll be okay."

After a pause, he said, "So what's the favor?"

I filled him in on my inadvertent attendance at Clayton's wake and the resulting hidden evidence. "Do you think you could make an anonymous call to the police department for me?"

"How do you get yourself into these things?"

"It seems to be a talent of mine. The thing is that Roy and Johnna's voices are too distinct. They have a recognizable something — an accent or cadence, and it's a small town. I can't ask one of them to call. Logan would pass out before he got the phone number dialed. You're my only hope."

"Okay. I'll call right now. But, Cam? You have to do me a favor."

"What's that?"

"Let me walk the dogs every now and

then. I'm going to miss hanging out with those guys."

I glanced around at my pack. Colby and Jack were playing tug-of-war with a rope, Isobel was warning off Gus by showing her teeth while he teased her by getting too close to her spot by the fridge. Little Liam was snuggled up in Brutus's blanket that Ben had situated in the corner of the family room the night before.

They were more than one person, or even two, could handle, but I wouldn't trade them for anything. "You're welcome to them anytime," I told Andy, who'd done his share of filling in holes the boys had dug in the backyard.

When we hung up, I felt better. Relieved. I hadn't told him about Lana's moonshine, because Ben didn't have a warrant for Lana's personal property. And who knew if it was even related to Clayton and the moonshine Ben was searching for. Lana could've just tucked it down farther in her bag as a reaction to hearing he was looking for moonshine. I couldn't go jumping to conclusions.

My phone rang before I set it back down on the table. I didn't recognize the number calling. "Hello?"

"Hello, Mrs. Hayman, this is Bob from

Bob's Sled Dogs. How are you today?"

"Good, thanks," I said, hoping that Soapy had called and canceled his teams for the race that was scrapped after Dixon's murder.

"I'm very sorry for the tragedy causing your festival to be canceled. I hope the town is recovering from the shock."

"We're a strong community," I said. "We'll pull through."

"I'm sure you will. Um, when exactly do you think that might be? We need to reschedule."

"Reschedule? Oh, I don't think we're going to pick up the festival where we left off. Maybe next year."

"Well, see, that causes a problem with our contract. I don't mean to sound callous, considering what transpired, but we'll need to be paid in full whether our teams race or not. We reserved that day for your festival and weren't able to book another event with the short notice. Maybe you want to discuss it with Soapy and get back to me?"

"I didn't realize," I said, trying to recall the contract I'd signed. "I'll have to call you back."

Bob apologized one last time and we hung up. On one hand, I'd budgeted for his teams to come out and race, but on the other hand, it wasn't like we canceled on account of rain. A man was murdered at the ice sculpting event. The town Olympian, for goodness sake. There was no way the festival could go on after that.

But a contract was a contract. I'd have to see what Soapy wanted to do.

I wished I had work to do while I waited for my fate with Ben, but the next event in town wasn't until Field Days at the high school in spring. I ambled into the front room and looked out the window. Fat, fluffy snowflakes drifted lazily down from the sky. The sun was shining, reflecting light off the frozen canal. A small group of searchers rambled along the opposite side in front of Read and ReRead still hoping to find Mike. They were led by Carl Finch who carried a tall, ornate walking stick, and knowing him and his predilection for religious relics, it might have once belonged to Moses or one of the prophets.

I hadn't talked to my mom in a little over a week. As far as I knew she still talked to Carl, but their relationship wasn't exclusive. She said it was because she just got divorced and anyway she lived two hours away from Carl. They were just having fun. When they were together though, they seemed totally enamored of one another. My parents' divorce was still something I was letting sink in, so Mom dating was like aliens landing in my backyard. I did my best to act interested in her personal life and not let the thought of her dating upset me.

Dad told me he wasn't interested in dating. He was enjoying the single life, traveling everywhere he'd always wanted to go that my mother didn't want to. Like Egypt. He was currently enjoying the pyramids while smoking cigars, something else Mom never allowed him to do. Every now and then he texted me a selfie he'd taken, but I could never see the background since his face took up the entire screen. I imagined he was somewhere amazing, though. I had to get Mia to teach him the fine art of taking selfies.

So it seemed they were both enjoying the single life.

Which brought me back to thoughts of my own predicament — Ben walking through the door and what he would say about me snooping at Clayton's wake.

It was dark when I woke to the front door opening and the dogs taking off to find out who was home. I'd fallen asleep on the couch reading with Gus curled up at my feet, Liam dozing in the crook of my arm, and Colby and Jack in a pile of drooling, snoring fur on the floor beside me.

"Ben?" I called, sitting up.

"No," Mia said. "And why haven't you answered any of my texts?"

"I was asleep. What time is it?"

"Seven. Where's Dad?" She stood in the archway between the foyer and front room, kicking her boots off her feet. Snow was flying all over the place. Gus was jumping around trying to catch it in his mouth.

"I don't know. I thought he'd be home hours ago."

I rubbed my eyes, disoriented, like I'd slept through an entire day. This morning seemed like it happened yesterday.

"Betty's been trying to reach you," she said. "Is your cell phone turned off or something?"

"No."

"When was the last time you charged it?" She tilted her head and her eyebrows shot up, like she was the adult scolding the teenager for not answering her call.

"It might be dead," I admitted. I always forgot to plug it in. Batteries shouldn't have to be charged. I never had to plug in my TV remote and it ran on batteries. Of course, before we canceled our landline, I always hung up the cordless phone on the base to charge, so I guess it did make some kind of sense, but whatever. "What did Betty want?"

"How should I know? She just asked me why she couldn't reach you. I figured she'd stop over."

"It must not have been too important then." I stood and stretched. "Did you have dinner?"

"I'm not hungry," she said, turning and bolting up the stairs toward her bedroom with Liam at her heels bounding after her.

I wandered into the kitchen, wondering if Ben would be hungry when he got home. I took a pack of chicken from the freezer and tossed it in the microwave to defrost. He must've found something at Clayton's house to be delayed getting home.

My wrist throbbed, so I dug through my bag for the prescription pain pills, chasing the rattling sound around the bottom. My hand wrapped around a flat, round container. I didn't know what it was, but was certain it wasn't the cylinder shape of a pill bottle. I finally found it, and taking it out, realized the child-proof cap was also Cameron-proof with my hand wrapped like a mummy and stuck in a sling. This was the first time I'd been without Monica or Ben since breaking my wrist.

"Mia?" I shouted. "Mia!"

155

The only reply was the faint beat of music straining down from her bedroom. She couldn't hear me. I'd just wait for Ben to get home.

When the microwave beeped, I took the pack of chicken out, placed it on the counter, and cut the plastic wrap with a knife. Cooking one-handed would be difficult, but not impossible.

Who was I kidding? Cooking was difficult for me at the best of times. This was going to be a disaster.

I got a pan out and put it on the stove then poured some oil in it and turned the burner on. When I picked up a chicken breast, it was still frozen in the center and stuck to the one beside it, which was stuck to the one beside that, and so on. So I tried to shake them apart.

When that didn't work, I tried to pry them apart by slipping a knife between them, but all I managed to do was slide the whole pack across the counter. So I picked them up again and tried shaking them apart again.

"Good gravy, come apart," I muttered, getting more frustrated by the second, and shaking them harder and harder.

Ever the helpers, Colby and Jack began barking encouragement and jumping around my legs. "No," I told them. "Stop.

Go lay down."

The smell of burning oil drew my attention back to the stove, where smoke was wafting out of the pan. Sensing my distraction, one of the cheese twins leapt up and snagged the chicken from my hand. The two thieves darted underneath the kitchen table and started a raucous game of tug-of-war with my dinner!

I flipped the burner off, but it was too late. The fire alarm started blaring in the hallway, sparking a chorus of barking from every corner of the house. Mia's music got louder, and a couple seconds later she ran into the kitchen. "What's going on?" she asked, frantic.

"I'm making dinner," I shouted over all the noise, because that explained it all.

I opened a window and Mia opened the patio doors, waving her hands around to clear the air.

"I'm home!" I heard Ben yell from the front door. He strode into the kitchen like he wasn't surprised at all to find me and Mia standing in a haze of smoke with the fire alarm going off. He opened the basement door and disappeared behind it, returning a minute later with the step ladder. We watched as he disabled the smoke detector, leaving only the sound of Mia's music playing upstairs.

"Making dinner, Cam?" he asked with a smirk. "You shouldn't have."

The twins bolted out from under the table and lunged out the patio doors. Gus and Liam followed, hoping for a scrap of the chicken that was long gone.

"Cooking with one hand isn't easy," I said in my defense.

"You didn't need to cook. I brought home Chinese food." He picked up a bag he'd set on the table in the foyer and brought it into the kitchen. "I know you can't cook with your arm in a sling. I'll take care of that end of things." He pulled me in for a hug and motioned for Mia to join us. "My crazy girls," he said, kissing Mia on top of her head.

His easy acceptance of the chaos was unexpected. The Ben I used to live with would've reacted like a raging bull, coming home to this after a long, hard day at work. And why wasn't he angry with me — or at least suspicious of my motives — for being at Clayton's during the wake?

"Why don't you go turn that music off and we'll eat dinner?" he said to Mia. She skipped up the steps, and Ben turned to me. "How's the wrist?"

"I can't open my pill bottle," I said, picking it up from the counter and handing it to him. "Mind helping me out?"

"Not at all." He twisted the top off. "Speaking of pill bottles," he said, opening the cupboard door and taking out a glass. "You wouldn't know anything about an anonymous call to the police instructing them to tell me that there was a bottle of blood pressure pills tucked between Clayton's couch cushions right where you were sitting today, would you?"

He filled the glass with water and sat it on the counter beside me. I busied myself with swallowing the pain pill. Finally, I asked, "Were the pills what you were looking for?"

"They were one of the two brands of blood pressure pills in Clayton's system at the time of his death. The pills I found in the couch were his. His doctor prescribed them."

"Was his name on the bottle?" I asked. I'd never had a chance to look before shoving the bottle between the cushions.

"There was no label."

"Where would he have gotten another kind then? And why would he be taking them?"

Ben shook his head. "I don't know."

"Did you find the moonshine you were after?"

"No. I found some, but it ended up being a lower proof than what the toxicology report showed. It wasn't the moonshine in his system when he died."

"Mysterious pills and moonshine. Interesting."

"What we do know is that the wheat flour isn't what killed Clayton. Old Dan and Frank are being released. All of the other food in Clayton's kitchen is being tested."

"That's a relief," I said. "Dan and Frank will be happy to get home and back to work at the mill."

The gate house would be empty again.

And Andy still wouldn't have a job.

"Cam, I know you and Monica weren't just being good neighbors by going over to Clayton's today. You're going to have to tell me what you were up to, but right now I just want to forget about all of it and have a relaxing dinner with you and Mia."

Something else was going on. Ben never let his investigations go, not even after a hard day. He always brought work home with him.

"There's something you're not telling me," I said. "What is it?"

He looked down at his hands, resting on the counter. "No, I won't talk about this here. Not now. When I come home, I'm going to leave it all at the door. I told you things would change if I came back home."

"I don't want you to bury your feelings, though." I reached out and took his hand. "You can talk to me. I know your job isn't like going to an office and punching out at five o'clock."

Ben looked up at me with haunted eyes.

"What happened?" I asked. "This isn't about moonshine or blood pressure medication. Tell me."

"I found something else stashed away under that couch, Cam."

I felt my pulse begin to race. "What?"

"An ice pick."

His words lingered in the air around us. It took my brain a minute to accept them and take hold. "No," I whispered.

Ben nodded. "Jason Banks murdered David Dixon."

TEN

Betty stood behind her bakery counter mixing ingredients in a huge bowl. "Lana called me all in a tizzy yesterday. She mentioned that you and Monica had been at Clayton's house when Ben arrived with the search warrant. I tried to call you but couldn't reach you."

"My phone was dead," I said, hoping she didn't ask what we were doing at Clayton's.

"I can't believe Jason would kill David Dixon," she said, breaking eggs into her bowl. "What reason would he have? David and Jason's dad were good friends."

"Well, Jason threatened me because I was going forward with the festival after Clayton's death, and I barely even knew the man. Dixon was hosting the events and he was one of Clayton's best friends. I can only imagine how angry that made Jason."

"But angry enough to kill him? It doesn't make any sense."

"Ben and Sheriff Reins will get to the bottom of it."

"I hope they find Clayton's killer while they're at it. There's no way Jason killed his father, and having two killers in Metamora at the same time is too frightening to think about. Cass and Judy are considering closing their inns for a while, and want me to go on a vacation with them to get away from here until all of this blows over. But they can't afford to close their doors, and I know I can't. A three-generation vacation does sound nice, though."

"A vacation from the ice and snow as well as everything that's going on would be wonderful." I picked at a cranberry orange muffin Betty had given me with a cup of coffee, and swiveled on the stool beside her register. "Florida sounds perfect right now."

"I spoke to Richard last night. He and Robin will be staying in town until this whole situation is solved. He offered us use of their house in Lexington while they're here. It's not Florida, but it's a few degrees warmer at least."

The door opened with a jingle of the bell attached to the top, and Roy sauntered in. "Morning, ladies," he said.

"Morning, Roy." Betty put down her mixing bowl and wiped her hands on her apron.

"What can I do for you?"

"I was wondering what you do with the broken cookies, or your day-old items."

"Reverend Stroup usually comes by and collects them for the soup kitchen. Why?"

"Oh, times are getting tough, that's all," he said, waving his hand like it was no big deal.

"Do you need food, Roy?" I asked. "I'll take you to the grocery and get you some. You do so much for the Action Agency, it's the least I can do for you."

"No, no," he said. "I'm getting by. I don't need no charity."

I nodded, knowing I'd talk to him about it privately later.

"I'll let you ladies get back to your gabbing," he said and turned to leave.

"Take a cookie, Roy." Betty scooped a few warm ones off of a baking sheet and tucked them into a cellophane bag. "Hot from the oven."

"I think I will, then," he said. "They smell like Heaven."

"Taste like it, too," I said.

He held the bag up, nodded in thanks, and strode out the door.

"That was odd," Betty said. "I know he gets retirement pay from the Army. It must not be much, but he's never come in asking for day-old baked goods before."

"I didn't know Roy is an Army veteran. He doesn't talk about himself to me."

"He's a war vet. He served in Vietnam and doesn't talk about it ever. He came back and started drinking and that was that."

It explained a lot about Roy. I wanted to do something for him, a gesture big enough to be a thank-you for his service. He'd never let me, so it would have to be anonymous.

"Anyway," Betty said, resuming her mixing and our conversation. "Richard doesn't know what to think about Jason's arrest. Jason's been nothing but hostile and volatile since he and Robin got here. Only one thing is for certain: Clayton and David got on someone's bad side."

"What about Starnes?" I asked. "Is he being released? Is he afraid he's next? I mean, if the three of them were so close and two have been killed, it only stands to reason . . ." I lifted my eyebrows, indicating where my thought process was headed.

"I think that's why Lana is so frantic. She'd rather have him in jail where nobody can get to him, but he'll be released now, just like Old Dan and Frank."

"Betty," I said, easing my way into my next question, "Lana had a bottle of what I think was moonshine yesterday in her handbag. When Ben showed up asking if Clayton had any in the house, she shoved it down in her bag, hiding it. Do you think that's what Ben was looking for?"

Betty chuckled. "Probably, but he didn't die from moonshine, I can tell you that much. He'd been drinking moonshine made by Starnes for most of his life."

"Starnes makes moonshine?"

"What do you think he was doing with that copper tubing when we were at their house the other day? Not fixing the furnace, that's for sure. And Lana wasn't making up a giant batch of corn bread in that enormous pot on the stove, either."

"I didn't think anything of it," I said. "It wasn't suspicious at all."

"You didn't grow up around it like I did. Everyone in the older generation around here made moonshine. They used to sell it at the grist mill right out in the open. Old Dan had it sitting on the counter next to the dime candy and peanuts."

"It's illegal, though," I said, a niggling of an idea coming to mind. "Do you think David and Clayton threatened to out Starnes for making it? Does Starnes sell it, too?"

"Of course he does. How do you think they keep that wheat farm going? Farmers don't make much money, Cam. But Clayton and David wouldn't have any reason to expose Starnes's moonshine business. He's been doing it for years. Besides, they got free 'shine."

"There has to be a reason someone would want them dead."

"I can't think of what it would be." She sighed and set her wooden spoon down. "This used to be a nice, quiet town. Now we have to look over our shoulders and lock our doors. It's not the Metamora I know."

I wanted to tell her everything would be okay, but I wasn't sure it was the truth. The town wasn't what it once was. The whole world was changing, and it seemed to me that Metamora, unfortunately, was changing, too. For better or for worse.

When I needed to get my mind off of things, there was nothing better than taking a few monsters for a walk.

Gus took the lead, with Colby and Jack trailing behind, jumping around one another and tangling their leashes. Isobel only let Monica put a leash on her, so I left her home curled up with Liam napping beside the fridge.

I decided to walk across the bridge and toward Johnna's house, which was opposite of my normal dog-walking route, thinking

I'd search for Metamora Mike. My dogs always had a thing for Mike, sniffing him out and barking like mad when they caught sight of him.

The snow still covered the ground, but there was much less than a few days earlier. The slush had turned to ice and then softened again to a milkshake consistency that soaked through my canvas boots.

Gus stopped at the horse stalls and snuffled around the ground, digging his nose into the hay for a good sniff, while the twins attempted to dart across the street to the train depot where Jim Stein was standing outside smoking a cigar.

"Afternoon, Cam," he called. "Got your hands full there."

Struggling to keep two dogs restrained by holding their leashes in my right hand, and Gus's leash in the crook of my left elbow under the sling. I had to agree. "They rarely want to go the same direction."

"Searching for Mike?" he asked, blowing smoke into the air.

"I thought we'd give it a try while we were out anyway. Where do you think he's gone?"

Jim shook his head. "I fear the worst has happened."

A pang struck me in the chest. "But he's survived so many winters."

"Nothing like this has come through here in a long time."

I peered down the bank at the frozen canal. There was no denying that this winter had been worse than any others I'd experienced in town.

"He's only a duck, after all," Jim said. "But if he is around and you want to find him, you should play your clarinet. He seemed to like that."

The humiliating memory of Jim's wife, Fiona, teaching me to play in the train depot, and me making nothing but horrid goose honks on the clarinet, came flooding back to me. Mike had come waddling in the open depot door honking right back at me.

"I think he thought it was some kind of mating call," Jim said. "It could work to get him to come around if he's out here somewhere." He winked. "Give it some thought."

I told him I would and we headed off. It wasn't a bad idea, but the last time I played was in the fall, for my bees, and Fiona heard me playing across the canal. She wasn't exactly complimentary about my progress. But if worse came to worst, I'd do it to find Mike.

We approached Johnna's house on our right just as Roy was coming out of her door with a paper grocery bag. I saw a rolled up, crinkled potato chip bag sticking out of the top. Was Johnna giving him food from her cupboards?

Gus barked and they both looked over. "Are you following me, Cameron Cripps-Hayman?" Roy asked.

"She's got better things to do than follow some old coot around town," Johnna said. "You heard about Jason?" she called to me.

I led my troop to the bottom of her porch steps. "Betty just told me. Do you think he did it?"

" 'Course he did," Roy said. "They found the murder weapon in his house, didn't they? Sure sign of guilt right there."

"Doesn't seem right, though," Johnna said, scratching her chin. "He didn't have a reason to do it. What does Ben say about it?"

"Nothing. He doesn't tell me very much about cases."

Johnna narrowed her eyes. "Your mama never taught you how to get what you want from your man?"

Good gravy. My mom telling me things like that? The thought made me ill. Clearly, Mom was a free woman and out having the time of her life; I just didn't need to think about it.

"I better get going," I said, and tugged Gus's leash to get him moving. Colby and Jack were ready to head home. I knew when the cold started getting to them — they stopped being rowdy and actually walked like good dogs on their leashes. Soon I'd take them to Quinn for training. Now that they had names there was no reason not to.

On our way back to Ellsworth House, I wondered if Gus had what it takes to be a K9 officer like Brutus. I'd have to ask Ben what he thought about it. If Quinn could train Brutus to be a respectable police dog, then surely Gus could be one, too.

"Cameron?"

I turned to find Roy hustling after me.

"What's in those dog treats your sister makes?"

"There are all different kinds," I said. "All the ingredients are natural and come from the local stores and farms. Why? You don't have a dog. You're not thinking of eating them yourself, are you? Roy, let's go to my house and drop off the dogs and I'll take you shopping."

"No, no. I already told you I don't need anything. I was just curious is all. Johnna talks those treats up all the time and I wanted to make sure they were good for Charlie. He's her pride and joy, you know."

What was going on with Roy and Johnna? Certainly, they weren't becoming an item. Coconspirators was more like it. But he must have a soft spot for her. "I promise you they're good for Charlie. Monica uses fresh fruits, vegetables, cheeses, and meats, and mixes them in flour from the grist mill."

"Not that poisoned stuff that Clayton got his hands on, I hope."

"None of that, no," I said.

"I still don't understand how Starnes Buntly gets away with putting poisoned seeds in his flour, but I'm no lawman."

"It wasn't intentional," I said, "and it wasn't what Clayton died from, ultimately."

"How do they know it wasn't intentional? He was killed, wasn't he? Maybe it just didn't do its job."

"Why would Starnes want to kill Clayton? They were best friends."

"Most murdered people are killed by friends and family," he said. "There's always a reason why. We just need to find it."

"Do you know Richard Banks, Clayton's brother?"

"It's been a long time, but I used to know him when we were younger."

"Think you might want to stop over at Clayton's with me and express your sympathy?"

"You mean snoop? I'm free this evening. Pick me up at six o'clock."

And with that, he set off, up the road toward his house. I wrangled my dogs to the right and walked down the road beside the canal back home.

ELEVEN

This was a bad idea, and not just because I lied to Ben and told him I was taking Roy grocery shopping.

Roy had a hand-held tape recorder tucked in his pocket and had memorized a list of questions to work into the conversation. As we drove down the highway, he practiced a mock interview, as he called it.

"So then I'll say, 'It was mighty coincidental that you were on your way to town and your brother was murdered. You hadn't talked to him in years, had you? Had you? And out of the blue Dixon's murdered, and Jason's in jail, too. Who's staying in this house, then? You are, Richard. You killed them both, didn't you?' "

"You can't do that, Roy. He'll kick us out. You have to be subtle about this."

"Subtle, like an ice pick to the head, you mean?" He snorted and took a swig out of his flask.

"You really think Richard murdered his brother and Dixon?"

"I don't rule out anyone until I confront them with my suspicions."

"Confrontation isn't going to get us answers. Just follow my lead and don't say anything to make them boot us out the door."

"Fine, but you'll end up doing things my way. Mark my words."

We parked in the driveway and walked up the sidewalk, which, to my relief, was shoveled and salted. I didn't want to repeat the nasty fall I took here or at my own house.

Roy rapped on the door like he was a member of a CSI unit, and pressed Record on the tape recorder in his pocket. Richard answered and seemed truly surprised to see Roy.

"It's been a long, long time," he said, shaking Roy's hand. "Come in." He stepped back and gestured for us to come inside. "Robin's just stepped out to do some visiting of her own. She's at your mother-in-law's house," he said to me.

Paying the grande dame a visit. All who enter town must bestow their respects upon Irene Hayman. "How nice," I said, stifling an eye roll.

Ginger lifted her head from where she lay

beside the coffee table where the urn still sat. She was one depressed dog. Poor girl. I hoped she'd be okay soon.

"What brings you to town?" Roy asked, glancing suspiciously around the room.

"Originally, the plan was to visit my brother. Then it turned into burying him."

"But you had him cremated," Roy said, in his best *gotcha* voice. "Not buried."

"We're planning on burying the remains." Richard blinked with confusion. I could tell he was already beginning to wonder what Roy's ulterior motive was for being there. "I didn't realize you were friends with Clayton," he said.

"Small town," Roy said. "Who do you think killed him, then?"

"Um," I said, jumping into the conversation, "I talked with Betty today. She told me about Jason. I'm so sorry. Is there anything we can do for him, or for you and Robin?"

Richard's eyes moved back and forth between me and Roy, like he was trying to figure out if this was some sort of game. "Jason didn't kill anyone, especially not David Dixon, who'd been around him his whole life. Clayton, David, and Starnes used to take him fishing and hunting. He was like another father to Jason."

176

"What about the murder weapon?" Roy asked and pointed to the sofa. "Wasn't it found right under there?"

"What's this about?" Richard asked, crossing his arms. "You come in here and start throwing out accusations. What's the reason for this?"

"There's at least one murderer in town, maybe two," Roy said. "We're going to find out who it is and see that they're locked up for life."

"The two of you? Who appointed you to the FBI?"

"We appointed ourselves," Roy said, taking a step forward toward Richard, looking a bit menacing for an old drunk man.

"We shouldn't have come," I said, taking Roy by the arm. "I'm sorry. We're leaving."

"I want to get to the truth just as much as anyone else," Richard said. "That ice pick wasn't Jason's. There were other people here the day it was found, including you," he said to me. "How do I know you're not the killer and you tucked the weapon away under the sofa to frame Jason?"

"What? Why would I . . . ?" I shook my head in disbelief, but he was right. "Was anyone else here that day other than me, Monica, and Lana?"

"No, but the three of you are enough. One

of you must've done it."

"Well, it wasn't me or Monica," I said. "It had to have been Lana if it wasn't Jason's."

I remembered the way she shoved the bottle of moonshine deeper into her bag, and the way I had hidden the pill bottle in the couch. She could've done the same, rolling the ice pick right underneath at the same time I was tucking that pill bottle between the cushions.

"Lana loved Clayton like a brother," Richard said. "They'd known each other their whole lives, just like Starnes and David."

"Most murders are done by loved ones," Roy said, repeating his reasoning from earlier. "Which is why I'm interested in your whereabouts the morning of your brother's murder."

"I've put up with this nonsense long enough. It's time you leave." Richard stormed to the door and swung it open. "And don't come back."

I hustled through the door onto the porch. Roy took his time, like a peacock with his feathers furled, strutting past Richard. "Don't leave town," he said, lifting his chin. "We'll be in touch."

The door slammed behind us. I heard Ginger let out a few disgruntled barks from inside.

"That went well," Roy said, tugging on the bottom of his worn, navy blue polyester sports coat.

"Well? It was a nightmare."

We got back into the car. I wanted to yell at Roy, but the gears in my mind were working overtime. "I think he might have been on to something. What if the ice pick isn't Jason's after all?"

"Let's get some coffee and pie and discuss this further. There's a place right down the road here."

"How about a cheeseburger and fries instead? I could really go for McDonald's." It was my greatest weakness. I'd never give up my cheeseburgers.

"Even better."

I drove to the nearest one in Brookville. We went inside, ordered, and settled into a booth. "Going by Richard's theory," I said, "the ice pick had to belong to either Richard himself, Robin, Jason, me, Monica, or Lana. We can exclude me and Monica, of course."

"Can we?" Roy asked, cocking an eyebrow.

"Don't get smart," I said. "So that leaves the other four to consider."

"Robin's got no reason to kill David." Roy took a bite of his cheeseburger and wiped his mouth with the back of his hand. "She's

179

got a nice life in Lexington, and I don't see her having the guts to jab an ice pick into a man's head."

"I agree. I don't want to write her off completely yet, but she's the most improbable."

"Jason coulda done it, but the motive of him being mad at Dixon for being in the festival seems like a stretch."

"I saw firsthand how mad he was that the festival was even going to happen, so I'm not ready to let that one go yet."

"Fair enough, but I'm betting my money on Richard. Those two have been at odds for as long as they've been brothers."

I dipped a fry in ketchup, considering. "A lot of brothers bicker and don't get along. What makes you think it was more than that with Richard and Clayton? Enough to make Richard kill him?"

"He's always been a sly one. He's made a lot of money in his life by being in the right place at the right time. I have a feeling there's more to him coming up to visit Clayton than just brotherly love and forgiveness."

"Okay, so he stays on the list. What about Lana?"

"Can't see why she'd want Clayton dead. Heck, with him gone, half of the money she and Starnes make on moonshine is gone with him."

"Half? He drank that much?"

"Nah, but he used it to barter with. Gave them a lot of customers coming to get more when they found out where he got it from."

"So, essentially, he was advertising for them."

"Sure, if you want to see it like that."

"Then it doesn't really make sense for Lana to be the one who hid the murder weapon."

"None at all." He popped the last bit of cheeseburger into his mouth.

Still, I had something telling me not to write off Lana just yet. "I'll have to think about that some more."

"You do that."

"Roy, why didn't you ever tell me you're an Army veteran?"

He shrugged. "Didn't come up, I guess."

"Well, thank you for your service."

"How about one of them apple pies as a thank-you?"

"And a coffee to go with it?"

"You read my mind Cameron Cripps-Hayman. You read my mind."

By the time I got up the next morning, Mia was already at school, Ben was at work, and

Monica was baking up a storm in the kitchen. "I can't believe I slept until ten o'clock," I said, pouring myself a cup of coffee. "I can't remember the last time I slept this late."

"It's the weather," Monica said, rolling out a ball of dough. "I'd hibernate like a bear for the winter if I could get away with it."

"Thanks for letting me use your car last night."

"Anytime you need it, it's yours to use. You should probably look into getting one, though."

"I know. I will."

"You need something huge for all those dogs, like a big old Suburban."

"That's true. I'm going to ask Quinn when he can get them scheduled for training."

"He might be able to do it here. It's not like he isn't over all the time."

"Oh! The perks of having a sister dating a K9 trainer."

"Yes," she said, grinning. "Another one is a trip to Ireland. Well, that's a perk for me, not you. He's taking me to meet his family in the spring."

"Meeting the family all the way in Ireland? This is serious, Mon."

"It is. I think he's going to propose while we're there." Her shoulders hunched up and she let out a little squeak of excitement.

"I'm so happy for you!" I grabbed her and pulled her into a hug. "First a successful business, and now this."

"And all because I moved to this little no-stoplight town. I never would've guessed it."

"I told you, there's more here than fried chicken and antiques."

We laughed and the dogs got into the action, yipping and barking like they thought something was hilarious, too. Then a knock on the door sent them careening into the front hall.

"That's probably Johnna," Monica said. "She's picking up dog treats she asked me to make with crushed pretzels in them."

"Charlie is so spoiled," I said.

"I told her pretzels weren't a healthy option for dogs, but she insisted."

Monica let Johnna in and the two of them walked back into the kitchen. "Still in your jammies, Cam?" Johnna asked, shaking her head. "You missed the whole morning, didn't you?"

"I just need to put your treats into bags," Monica said.

"No need. I brought this plastic container

with me." She handed a bowl with a snap tight lid to Monica. "Might as well save the packaging for someone else."

"Want a cup of coffee?" I asked, being polite.

"No, thank you. I can't stay."

"Busy day?" I asked, wondering what Johnna was up to. She was the biggest gossip in town, which meant she always had information to share.

"Got some errands to run, and some people to see."

"What's the talk around town about Jason? Do people think he did it?"

Monica shot me a side glance, but Johnna didn't bat a lash. "Nobody thinks Jason killed David," she said. "It's ludicrous."

"Then who did it?" I sipped my coffee, like our conversation was about the weather. In a way, talking about murder was like talking about the weather now for the Action Agency. Unfortunately, it was becoming old hat for us.

"I'm just an old lady, what do I know?"

It wasn't the response I expected, not from Johnna. "You know a lot. You have to have some suspicion."

"Maybe I do. I don't know." She took the plastic bowl of treats from Monica and turned to head back to the front door. "I'll see what I can find out."

Who was she kidding? She had her ear to the ground and her nose to the wind and was practically a lightning rod for the talk in town. If anyone would hear what was being said, it was Johnna.

As she left, I wondered why she was acting so strange lately. Almost like she was keeping something from me. First Anna pulled away, and now Johnna. What would happen to our team if we couldn't lure them back in?

I wasn't fooling myself to think it would last forever. Anna and Logan were graduating in a few months and would leave for college. Johnna and Roy were older and even though they had time to spend with the Action Agency, they might want to sit back and enjoy being retired.

I was faced with knowing that I might need to find a new crew someday to help with town events and the occasional mystery. It wasn't something I liked to think about.

"What's wrong?" Monica asked, eyeing me with a worried expression.

"Just thinking about how fast things can change."

"Change isn't something to fear," she said. "I'm proof of that."

"That's true," I said, smiling. "Change has been nothing but positive for you."

"And Mom and Dad," she said. "Like it or not, they're both very happy now that they're not together."

"Yeah." I looked into the bottom of my empty coffee cup.

"And you," she said.

I looked up at her. She put her hand on my arm in the sling. "You have Ben and Mia, this beautiful home, a town full of friends, and a job you love even if it's the craziest job in the world."

It was true. Things would always change, but so far, change had been good to me. "We're pretty lucky, aren't we?"

"Very lucky," she said, leaning her head against mine. "Now help me make another three batches of treats."

I dug in, mixing dough with my good arm and filling her in on what I'd learned about the murders in the last day or so.

"I think Roy might be on to something," she said.

"With Richard? What makes you think that?"

"Well, if he's an opportunist who never got along with his brother, there might be a connection. He might have something to gain."

"But that's all speculation at this point. Jason owns the house. As far as I know, Richard didn't inherit anything from Clayton's death."

"As far as you know." She pointed a wooden spoon at me. "I think it needs to be looked into more. What do you know about Clayton's possessions?"

"Nothing. I mean, nothing other than he owned his house and property. And of course, what came out the day he was killed about the hill on his land being a Native American burial mound."

"Okay, so start there. What would that mean for Clayton that Richard might stand to benefit from?"

"My mind goes straight to John Bridgemaker and Paul Foxtracker, but I know they didn't kill Clayton. They aren't even suspects this time, thankfully. I can't believe they were ever suspects in Butch Landow's murder just because they wanted to buy his farm to build a casino."

"What ever happened to that idea, anyway?" she asked, cutting bone shapes into the dough.

"I don't know. They haven't found land that I've heard."

In the silence that fell between us, I knew we were thinking the same thing. Call it

187

sisterly intuition.

"Clayton owned a Native American burial mound," she said, not even looking up from her cookie cutter.

"Someone stands to make a lot of money if they sell that land," I said.

"Do you know for sure that Jason inherited that property?"

"I don't know anything for sure," I said, wiping my hand on a tea towel. "But I plan to find out."

"You need to borrow my car?" she asked, smirking.

"When I do, I'll put gas in it." I said. "And help you make more treats."

"I'll leave the keys on the hall table."

"Thanks, Mon."

"Cam, just be careful. Whoever did this has already killed two people. Don't let anyone catch you snooping around."

"Don't worry. There's one person I haven't talked to yet who knows everything about this town, and he's not going to kill me. Soapy. I'll be back soon."

"Alright. Just do me a favor? Change out of your pajamas first, okay?"

I looked down at the flannel pants and sweatshirt I'd slept in, and laughed. The dogs started their yippy laughter again, bounding around us.

Good gravy. "Maybe I'll have another cup of coffee first."

TWELVE

Soapy was in the back room concocting a coffee bean, goat milk soap, a new product for them to sell. "I've tried and tried to make one of these over the years, but I haven't been able to get it right. It's the first soap I tried to make when we opened. I wanted it to be our signature soap. One of these days, I'll get it right."

The combination of both of the product lines they were known for seemed like a logical idea. "Bob from the bobsled team called me," I said. "We have to pay him even though we canceled, or reschedule."

"We'll reschedule then. I'm not paying for nothing."

"I'll find a date that works. I should probably wait until after the murders are solved, though. It might seem insensitive otherwise."

"You're probably right. I was so looking forward to that hockey match, too. Maybe we'll reschedule that as well."

"Do you think Jason Banks really killed Dixon because he was angry that he went ahead with hosting the festival?"

Soapy put down the tweezers he was using to strategically place coffee beans into the soap mold, and leaned back from the counter. "That boy has had a hot head ever since he was little. Now, that doesn't mean I think he killed anyone, but it doesn't mean I don't. It's a tough call to make, and all I know is that they found the ice pick under his sofa."

"I've been thinking about that ice pick, and about Clayton's death. Who would want to kill him? Who had something to gain from it?"

"Who says anyone had something to gain?"

"There has to be a motive, right?"

"A motive, yes, but where are you going with this, Cameron?" He pushed his glasses up farther on his nose, eyeing me.

"How would I find out about Clayton's house? His property? Did Jason inherit it? Was there a will?"

He shook his head. "If there wasn't a will, then Jason inherits everything as his only child. If there was a will, then I can't be sure who got the house."

"If he had a will, what are the odds he left anything to his brother?"

"Well, I tell you what, if he did leave something to Richard in his will, he was blackmailed to do it. Those two have had bad blood between them since high school when Richard took Robin from Clayton."

"What? Robin and Clayton?"

"Ah, it was a long time ago." He picked his tweezers back up. "Puppy love."

"But it's what caused the rift between them?"

"As far as I know, it is."

"I got the impression that he met her in Kentucky."

"Oh, no. She's from Metamora, too, but briefly. Her family moved here and then away again after only a year."

"And she and Richard stayed together?"

"Well, they must have." He chuckled.

I tapped my fingers on the counter. "Something doesn't add up."

"Murder never does add up," he said.

"In the end the motive becomes clear, though. So far, nothing is clear to me about any of this."

"Maybe you're looking too closely. Maybe if you stand back a bit and look from another angle?"

I nodded. Maybe he was right. Maybe I

was trying to fit pieces together that weren't even part of the puzzle.

"If you must investigate on your own — and I know you have a good track record to stand by — take it one step at a time. If there's a connection between the murders, it'll reveal itself."

"That's good advice. Thanks, Soapy."

"I believe that secrets want to be found out, which is why they usually are." He picked up a bar of soap wrapped in the Soapy Savant packaging. "Theresa made this. Citrus and sage. It smells good enough to eat." He handed it to me. "Take that home with you and have a nice soak. I always do my best thinking in the tub."

I bought a hot peach ginger tea with honey before I left and decided to stop in to Read and ReRead next door to see Brenda. She was reading a children's book to a circle of five preschoolers when I walked in the door. I sat down in a comfy chair between two of the book stacks to wait.

Sipping my tea, I perused the shelves beside me. On my right was a section on local history, books written by townspeople over the years that weren't for sale, only for reference. There was a book written on the grist mill, one on the founders of Metamora, and another on the schoolhouse next door to Ellsworth House. I pulled the one about the schoolhouse off the shelf and started flipping through it.

I found a list of students that included Daniel Gardner — Old Dan — and Elaina Nelson, aka Grandma Diggity. Few other last names stood out. Brooks, who would be an ancestor of Fiona Stein, and Ellsworth, ancestor of my husband on his maternal side of the family.

Scanning through a list of teachers I came across Cordelia Banks, the first female teacher at the school. She could be an ancestor of Clayton, Richard, and Jason. I wondered just how long the Banks family had lived in Metamora, and more importantly, how long they'd owned the property with the burial mound. Had there been some Hatfield and McCoy type of feud brewing over the decades due to the ownership of that land?

"Hello!" Brenda said, popping around the corner of the stacks. "I'm finished with story time. What are you reading?"

"The history of the schoolhouse. Do you know where I can find pubic records for Metamora?" I stood up and slid the book back on the shelf.

"Probably at the Franklin County Court House, why?"

194

"I'm just curious about that Native American burial mound Clayton Banks owned."

"You think it has something to do with his murder?"

"I don't know, but I'm leaving no stone unturned."

"Well, I think you can find all of the public records online. Do you want me to help you look?"

"I'll take any help I can get."

I followed Brenda to the main area of the store. She pointed to a table. "Go ahead and sit there. I'll get my laptop."

Brenda set up her laptop on the table, and I rifled through my bag for a pen and paper. "What do I hear? Breath mints?" she asked.

"That or my pain pills rattling around."

"Are you still in pain?"

"No, but I haven't taken the bottle out of my purse yet."

"When do you get a hard cast?"

"I have to go back tomorrow morning."

"Can I be the first to sign it?"

I smiled at her. "If you can beat the people I live with."

"Okay, I'll settle for first nonresident of Ellsworth House to sign it."

Brenda pulled up the page for public records and we began to weed through. After about twenty minutes of not finding much, she said, "One of those ancestry websites might be easier to use. Sometimes they link to legal documents. There's a lot of legal mumbo jumbo on here."

"Let's try that."

After only a few minutes on the ancestry site, we found the Banks family tree that ran through Metamora. "Cordelia is listed in the schoolhouse history book. She was the first female teacher in town."

"Let's see who she married." Brenda clicked on Cordelia's name, expanding the tree. "Earnest Banks. They had seven kids! Boy people had big families back then."

"Do you see anything linking to a property deed?"

"Nothing tying them to that address yet." She followed different rabbit trails down the Banks family line. The door opened, and two women came inside. "I'll be right back," she said.

"That's okay," I told her. "I've taken enough of your time. It was just an idea I had."

"I'll keep looking and let you know if I find anything."

Brenda greeted her customers, and I took my leave. I could do what would be easy and ask John and Paul the history of the land. I was certain they would know. But I didn't want to drag them into it. They'd been the objects of suspicion enough in the past few months, and I was the wife of the town's police officer. If I went around asking them questions, they might get the wrong idea.

Something was sure to turn up soon. A clue, a motive, or an idea in my brain. In the meantime, I'd take Soapy's advice and have a nice long soak in the tub with my new bar of soap.

Ben helped me into my coat the next day. "You don't have to come with me," I told him. "I can take Monica's car. I know you have a ton of work to do."

"I'm coming with you to get your cast put on," he said, slipping the sling back over my head. "Work can wait a few hours." He turned to Brutus. "You're in charge. Don't let that cat sneak in."

"Good luck with that," I said, laughing. "The dogs never even know when Spook's in the house."

"He's probably all curled up in Finch's castle, anyway."

"I know I would be. I mean, if I were that cat." I sneered. "Or my mother."

Ben let out a sharp laugh. "I'm glad you're not either of those."

We went out to the driveway and he helped me up onto the passenger seat of Metamora One. "Still no sign of Mike?" I asked, hoping he'd heard something.

"Nobody's seen him. Don't worry, he'll show up in the spring. He's a smart duck."

On our way out of town, we passed Roy's trailer. I pointed and told Ben that was where he lived. "Did you know he's a retired Army vet?"

"I was born here, Cam, and Irene Hayman's my mom. I know all about everybody." He grinned and shook his head.

"Right, of course you do. The only way you'd know more is if Johnna was your mom."

"Then I'd be broke from bailing her out of jail every time she steals a ball of yarn."

"Speaking of broke, I think Roy is. Johnna's been giving him food. I've seen her do it twice now, and he came into Betty's asking for day-old bakery items."

"Well that's strange. He has enough to spend in the Cornerstone bar every night. If he was having trouble, Carl, Jim, and those guys would know and help him out with money."

"Maybe they don't know."

Ben's brows drew in. "I'll ask around. Johnna can't afford to feed him and herself, that much I'm sure of." He patted my knee. "I'll get to the bottom of it."

We got to the professional building attached to the hospital where the doctor's office was. We sat in a giant waiting room that was used by all the doctors in the building. We didn't have to wait long before we were ushered to a room by a nurse. "I have to apologize," she said, starting out making me feel not so comfortable about this experience. "We only have one color of fiberglass tape left. Our new supply comes tomorrow if you'd like to reschedule."

I let out a sigh of relief. "It's okay. I don't care what color it is."

"Great, I'll let the doctor know. He'll be right in."

Ben looked at me with a sly smile. "I hope its camouflage."

"Camouflage? Good gravy! I didn't know they had camouflage!"

"It's probably not a color they run out of either," he said, starting to chuckle.

"Ben! What if I have a camouflage cast? This is serious!"

"You'll be all set for duck hunting." He laughed like he was watching Chris Rock on TV. "Get it? Mike."

"I get it." I couldn't help but laugh with him.

The doctor came in and looked at us with wide eyes and a huge smile. "Nobody's this happy on cast day," he said.

"My husband thinks he's a comedian," I said.

"He had you laughing," the doc said, "so maybe he found his calling."

"Don't encourage him, please."

We settled down and the doctor explained what would happen. "My orthopedic tech will come in and cast your arm, but first we'll want to take x-rays to make sure it's still aligned properly. We don't want it to mend crooked, do we?"

"Definitely, not."

"When I unwrap it and remove the splint, it's going to move your arm a bit. We'll do our best to keep it immobile, but it's going to give you some pain."

He wasn't lying. When they took the splint off, my arm felt like a rubber band being pulled all kinds of directions it wasn't supposed to go in. I gritted my teeth and tried not to cry.

The x-rays came back fine, so they went ahead with the cast. I lay on the exam table and closed my eyes tight, focusing on something other than the pain while the doctor held my arm in the correct position and the technician began to wrap it in the fiberglass casting tape. "Once we get the first layer on, it'll feel better," the tech said.

Ben held my other hand and stood behind my head, out of the way. "It'll be done soon," he whispered.

Even after the first layer of tape was applied I kept my eyes shut, determined to just get through the whole experience.

"It's not camouflage," Ben said, but I heard the humor in his voice.

"What color is it?" I asked, afraid to look.

"Let's just say it's the opposite of camouflage."

I didn't even want to think about what that meant. When the doctor and tech were done, I opened my eyes and saw nothing but highlighter orange. My arm was like the sun, a giant ball of fire.

"Wow," I said, sitting up. "That's bright."

"It's not forever," the doctor said. "We'll need you back here in a couple weeks to see how it's mending."

The cast reached my elbow, but I didn't need a sling anymore. I rebuffed Ben's attempts to help me with my coat and put it on myself without struggling for the first time in days. "Easy peasy," I said.

"You're a pro." He opened the door and we walked out through the office and back into the waiting room where I would schedule my follow up appointment.

A veritable army of medical receptionists sat in a row behind a long counter with half wall dividers. I sat in the chair at the first available spot with Ben standing behind me. As the receptionist searched the doctor's available appointment times, I overheard the woman beside her talking to a patient.

"You need to come in for a refill . . . Yes, I know you lost your blood pressure pills, but you didn't have any refills left, so you'll need to come in. How long has it been since you last took your medication? . . . About a week? . . . Okay, Mrs. Buntley let me look for a time to squeeze you in today. Please hold."

I jerked my head up to look at Ben. Had he heard the conversation? By the look on his face, he had. "Don't even think about it, Cam," he said. "I'll follow up on this."

"A little coincidental, don't you think?" I asked.

"Very."

Lana Buntley lost her blood pressure pills about a week ago, around the same time when a blood pressure medication that was not Clayton's was found in his system. Could Lana be Clayton's killer?

THIRTEEN

"She killed him," Monica said, tossing popcorn in her mouth. Ben was working late and Quinn was busy with bookkeeping, so she and I decided to go to see a movie on Friday night instead of staying home. "There's no other explanation."

I fought with the cellophane around my peanut M&M's box. "But where's the proof? I mean, what if she does take the same kind of medication that was found in Clayton's system and she lost her pills the same time he was murdered? How do we know he didn't take them and commit suicide? How do we know they were her pills in his system and she didn't just drop them at the hair salon or somewhere?"

"It fits too well. You know she did it. I know she did it. Now we just have to prove it."

"How?"

She tapped her fingers on the side of the

popcorn box. "I don't know yet."

We watched a romantic comedy about a woman who moved back to her small hometown and juggled her old high school sweetheart and the new guy in town. It was cute and funny, but not enough to draw my thoughts away from Lana. What would her motive be for killing Clayton?

Did Clayton and Starnes have a falling out and Lana was getting revenge? Did he know something about Lana and Starnes that they needed to keep quiet? Betty said it wasn't about the moonshine; that Clayton actually helped them get customers. Maybe he wanted a cut and threatened to turn them in to the cops if they didn't agree? It was a possibility.

"Hey," Monica said, nudging me. I realized the credits were rolling. "Did you see any of the movie, or were you too busy calculating and plotting, Miss Marple?"

"You know this will drive me crazy until I figure it out." I told her about the moonshine angle, and she agreed it was worth finding out about.

"You need to talk to Lana Buntley," she said.

"I can't just call her and ask her if she killed Clayton with her blood pressure pills, and if I tell her what I heard at the doctor's office, she'll know Ben's on to her and it might ruin his investigation."

"That's why you have to be sneaky about it."

"It's hard to be sneaky when you have a traffic cone around your arm," I said, holding up my cast.

"A glow-in-the-dark traffic cone. It was hard to see the movie screen with that beside me."

"Next time bring sunglasses."

We left the theater and got in Monica's car. "Why don't we drive by the car dealership while we're in Brookville?" she asked. "They're closed, but we won't be harassed by salesmen while we look around."

"Okay. Can't hurt to look." I really missed my ancient hatchback that saw me through college, my job, and a move to Metamora before Mia killed it. It was the only car I'd ever owned. I didn't even know where to begin when looking for a new one.

"Change is good, Cam," Monica said.

"I don't have an issue with change."

She seemed to think otherwise. "You definitely don't like it."

"Who does?"

The first dealership she stopped at had a chain blocking the entrance, but Monica pulled over to the side of the road anyway.

"We can step over it. I doubt anyone will mind if there are two women looking around at cars."

"Ben's going to have to get us out of jail tonight," I said. "I can feel it."

"Just tug your coat sleeve down over your day-glow cast and come on."

We hustled out of the car and over the chain. "This way," Monica called, hurrying around to the side of the building. "We'll start with the used cars."

"We'll end there, too. I can't afford a new one. I don't even think I can afford a used one."

"You have a job now. You can afford a car."

"Says the successful dog treat entrepreneur."

"Oh, please. I have to live in your house."

"Until Quinn whisks you away to Ireland and doesn't bring you back."

She stopped in her tracks. "Do you think he'll want to live there?"

"I was only kidding, Mon."

"But really, do you think he will?"

Standing under the bright lights of the dealership lot, panic seemed to take over her features. "He has a business here and he knows you do, too," I said. "Of course he's not going to want to move back to Ireland."

She blinked a few times, considering. "Yeah, why would he want to move back?" But she didn't sound convinced.

I wasn't, either. He'd always planned on going back before meeting Monica. What if they got married and had kids and he wanted to be near his family? What if she moved all the way to Ireland?

"You're right," I said. "I have a problem with change."

The panic started to slip back over her face, so I amended my statement. "I don't want a different car. I want my old one back."

"Oh," she said, "well, you can't have it back, so pick a different one."

We walked up and down aisles full of SUVs and minivans. Most looked just like the last. "They have no character," I said.

"Character? They don't need to have character. They need to get you from point A to point B."

"No," I said. "They bore me. I don't want any of these."

"They bore you?"

"Monica, a car is a commitment, like a spouse. You're going to be with that car for a long time. Maybe for the rest of your life. It needs to be The One."

She threw her hands in the air. "You're

not supposed to have one car for the rest of your life!"

"If I can, I will," I said.

"There's not one car on this lot that you like enough to commit to driving?"

I glanced around again, but nothing stood out to me. "It's not here."

"Sometimes I think you were adopted."

"Sometimes I do, too."

"All right, let's get out of here."

We made our way back to the chain, stepped over, and got in the car. Monica pulled her phone out of her pocket to see if Quinn had called or sent her a text message. "I forgot to take it off silent when we left the theater," she said.

"I forgot mine, too."

I opened my handbag and surprised myself by finding my phone sitting right on top of my wallet. No rummaging around required for once. I turned my ringer back on and noticed a text from Brenda.

I FOUND SOMETHING INTERESTING. CALL ME ASAP!

"Whoa," I said. "Brenda was helping me track the property records of Clayton's land, and she's found something." I dialed her number.

Monica turned toward me in anticipation. "Put it on speaker."

I nodded and hit the speaker button. It rang a couple of times and Brenda answered.

"Hey," I said. "I've got Monica here, too. What did you find out?"

"Nothing on the property. Something more interesting."

"What?"

"Jason's mom isn't Clayton's ex-wife."

"Who's his mom?"

"Robin Banks. *Richard's* wife."

"Holy!" Monica said, and covered her mouth with her hands.

"No wonder Clayton and Richard had a falling out," I said.

"How'd she end up with Richard, though?" Brenda asked. "Did Robin dump Clayton to be with his older brother? Is that why she left Jason with Clayton?"

"I don't know."

"I once heard my mom say that Clayton and his wife had the wedding and the baby backwards," Brenda said. "He must have gotten custody right from the start."

Monica nodded in agreement. "That seems like the most likely scenario. How do we find out?"

"More importantly," I said, "how does this tie in with his murder? Or does it tie in at all?"

"It might still have something to do with the property," Brenda said. "Robin might use that connection to convince him to sell. If it's a lot of money — millions — he'll most likely give them a cut. I'd help out my family if I got that much."

"Most people would," I said. "But would Jason want to help the mom who didn't raise him? It's a solid theory to look into."

We told Brenda thanks and goodbye and hung up.

"How do Lana and her pills fit into this?" Monica asked. "How would Robin or Richard kill Clayton with Lana's pills?"

"I don't know. There are a lot of threads that have to be knit together still."

"Is that where Johnna comes in? The knitting?"

"Ha ha. Very funny. I do need to find out what she and Roy think of these new developments, though. They have a lot of insight that I don't."

"Looks like the Metamora Action Agency is closing in on the case."

"I hope so." Soapy was right, secrets did want to come out, and as long as they kept giving themselves up, we'd find out what happened to Clayton and Dixon.

"I don't believe it," Roy said, dumping a

quarter of his flask into his coffee. "Anybody can put whatever they want on those computers and people believe it. Not me. I'm not falling for it."

"I'm on the website Brenda used," Logan said. We'd all convened at my house for a Saturday-morning meeting. "A photo of Jason's birth certificate was uploaded to his profile on the Banks family tree. It seems legit." He spun his laptop around to show us.

"Could be a forgery," Johnna said, looking up from her yarn and needles. "Clayton got married after Jason was already here, sure, but no one ever suggested his wife wasn't the mother. Of course, she wasn't from around here."

"Whether it's real or fake," Anna — who had shocked us all by showing up this morning — said, "Robin and Richard still have the same motive: the money from the property sale." She sat across the table from Logan and hadn't looked at him once.

"As long as people believe it," Roy said.

"As long as Jason believes it," Monica chimed in from behind the kitchen counter where she was mixing the first batch of treats for the day. "He's the key to them getting any money if he sells the land."

Gus was glued to Roy's side and kept

sniffing him, nudging his leg. "Gus, stop," I said. "What is with you today?"

"How do we even know John and Paul want that land?" Johnna asked.

"I'm sure if land that has an earth mound on it comes up for sale they'll buy it — or the association will," I said.

"What about Lana's pills?" Roy asked. "Seems like a more logical path to go down than worrying about who Jason's birth mom is and all this ancient business."

"How is that more logical?" Logan asked.

"When you hear hoof beats, think horse not zebra," he said.

"What does that even mean?" Anna said, taking his spiked coffee away from him.

"Listen, miss," he said, reaching for his mug, "you can't just show back up and start bossing me around."

"You've had enough of this," she said, getting up and darting to the sink. "I'm dumping it and pouring you a cup without the booze."

Roy rested his head on his hand, resigned. "Fine, but I liked these meetings better when you weren't around."

"Roy!" Johnna said, poking him with a knitting needle. "You say you're sorry."

"I'm not!" he barked, making Gus do the same. "Where's she been anyway? Not coming around and then thinks she can just show back up with no apology or explanation. Just because she's got boy troubles."

Monica gasped. Logan blushed a deep scarlet, and Anna dropped the mug into the sink and dashed for her coat.

"Wait," Logan pleaded, standing up. "I have something to say." His face drained of all color, going from red to a ghostly white. I said a silent prayer that he didn't pass out in my kitchen.

"So everyone knows," Logan began, "I want to explain myself and what I was thinking about me and Anna going to college. I didn't talk to her about it, or worry about it, because I had it worked out in my head already. I didn't think I needed to talk about it. But she didn't have it worked out the same way in her head."

"What did you have all figured out?" Anna asked, with only a slight edge to her voice.

"I took it for granted that we'd stay together no matter where you went to school. We'll be home for holidays and summers, at least to start, and we'd text and video chat when we were doing homework at night, like we've done all year. Or at least until I upset you."

Anna took a deep breath. "You can't just plan things in your head and think that everybody else is thinking the same, Logan. You have to communicate. That's what people do. We talk. Try it sometime."

"The fella just did that," Roy said. "Now it's you who's trying to cause a problem. Booze might not be good for me, but that high horse won't be good for you, girlie. Climb on down and give him a break."

Anna's chin quivered, her eyes got glassy and she blinked a few times. She was a strong young lady who was brilliant in her own right, and not used to being vulnerable to her emotions. "I'm sorry, Logan."

"You don't have anything to apologize for," he said. "I'm the one who didn't —"

"I was so mean to you," she said. "I know you don't get it sometimes, that relationship things need to be spelled out for you. I shouldn't have expected you to start a conversation about where ours was heading."

"No, it's my fault," he said. "I need to do better. I'll do better."

"Okay, kiddos," Johnna said. "Sounds like a truce to me. Let's get back to why we're here at the crack of dawn."

Anna and Logan sat back down, but it was clear from the googly eyes they were giving each other that being across the table wasn't going to work.

"Here," Roy said to Anna, standing up. "Take my chair and try not to make me sick with your lovey dovey junk."

They swapped seats, Gus right on top of Roy's every move, and Logan took Anna's hand. The smiles on their faces could've powered the town for a decade.

"So back to Lana," I said. "How does she fit in?"

"We need to find out where she thinks she lost those pills and when," Johnna said.

"How are we going to do that?" Roy asked, patting Gus's giant head as he sniffed him from toe to thigh. "Call her and say, 'We heard you lost your pills, think they found their way into Clayton's stomach?'"

My mind latched onto an idea. "Calling isn't a bad idea," I said.

"That was a terrible idea," Monica said.

"Just . . . hold on. I have a plan."

"One of Cameron's plans," Roy said. "This should be good."

I picked up the phone and asked Johnna for Lana's number. She knew everything, so surely she'd have that. Sure enough, she took a little address book out of her knitting bag and rattled off the phone number. I dialed while Logan looked up which county Hamilton, Ohio, was in.

When Lana answered, I tried to change

my voice enough for it to not be familiar, but not enough to sound like I was disguising it. "Is this Mrs. Lana Buntley?" I asked.

"Yes," she said.

"I'm calling from the Lost Drugs Recovery Department of Butler County. We've been informed that you've misplaced your blood pressure medication. Do you have any idea where you were when you misplaced it?"

"I don't know. The bottle was in my bathroom medicine cabinet, and then it was gone. I tried to recall if I put it in my purse to take with me. I do that sometimes, because I like to take the pills with food, so if we're going out for a bite to eat, I'll take them along, but I can't remember. Those pills could be anywhere."

"Do you recall the day you discovered they were missing?" I asked.

"What is the Lost Drug Recovery Department?" she asked, suddenly sounding suspicious.

"It's . . . um . . . it's the recovery effort of the county to . . . uh . . . recover lost drugs. Prescription drugs. It happens a lot. You'd be surprised."

"I am surprised. You don't think I sold them, do you?"

"Sold them? No. No. I don't believe . . . that is . . . we've found there isn't a market

216

for blood pressure medication drug deals. By individuals. Drug dealers. That kind of thing."

Anna covered her eyes. Roy got his flask out. Johnna twittered in almost silent laughter beside me.

"Anyway," I continued, "do you recall when you misplaced your medication?"

"I noticed when we were packing to spend some time in Indiana, a week ago now."

"And um, did you go to Indiana?"

"We didn't. What does that have to do with my lost pills?"

I frowned. The Buntleys *did* come to Indiana. Why was she lying? "Uh, nothing. I'm just getting a time line together."

"Well, that's all I know. If I find them, I'll let my doctor know."

"Thank you for your time, Mrs. Buntley. Goodbye."

I hung up and rehashed the whole conversation to everyone. "So she could've misplaced them at home, or taken them with her somewhere and lost them."

"No one saw Starnes or Lana in town before Clayton died," Johnna said. "So how would they get the pills to Clayton even if they are the mystery kind that was in his system?"

"Which we don't know," Logan said.

217

"Hoof beats," Roy said.

"I'll beat you," Johnna said.

"There are still too many unknowns," I said. "Nothing is adding up like it should."

"And what about David Dixon?" Anna asked. "Do we really think Jason killed him?"

We all looked from one to another around the table, but nobody seemed certain enough one way or another to say anything. Finally, Roy broke the silence.

"Hoof beats," he said. "Jason didn't do it. Lana's the most obvious, just like the pills."

"How is Lana more obvious than Jason?" I asked. "It was his couch the ice pick was found under."

"It's too coincidental," he said, taking a swig from his flask.

"Maybe we should split up," Logan suggested. "Half of us work on Dixon, and the other half on Banks. Anna and I will start finding info on Dixon. Who wants to help us?"

"I will," Monica said in a rush, like she was buzzing in on *Jeopardy.* I gave her a dirty look over my shoulder.

"Guess that leaves us," I said to Roy and Johnna. "Zebra hunters, or horse hooves or whatever."

"You're mixing up the saying," Roy said,

pushing Gus away. "Now I'm leaving. I've had enough of this dog prodding me with his nose."

"Gus!" I called. "Get over here! I'm sorry, Roy. I don't know why he's taken such an interest with you today. Unless you have bacon in your pockets or something."

"That reminds me," he said, "Soapy's started selling sandwiches. Think I'll go see if he's got any breakfast ones with bacon."

"That's the best idea I've heard all morning," Johnna said, tucking her knitting away in her bag. "I'll join you."

"Cameron?" Roy said. "You coming along? You're the third wheel on our investigative team, after all. We can leave these other three to their business. Not that they're going to solve anything without us."

"How much do you want to bet we find Dixon's killer before you guys find Clayton's?" Anna asked.

"Don't encourage him to gamble," Johnna said.

"Hush," Roy told her, then turned back to Anna. "You know I'm a wagering man. I'll bet you —"

"We're not betting!" I shouted, stopping the craziness before it got out of hand. Roy was taking food from Johnna; he was not making a bet with Team Anna and Logan.

Roy gave Logan a sly wink, like they'd finish their wager later, when I wasn't around. Gus nudged him in the hip, sending him off balance. He took a step and grabbed the back of the chair. "This dog needs to learn some manners!"

"Gus!" I yelled. "I'm sorry, Roy. I'll buy your breakfast sandwich to make it up to you."

"Better throw in a cup of coffee, too. You never know when this hip will give out on me now because of that."

"Absolutely. Coffee, too."

Good gravy. If I was the next to kick off in this town, everyone should know it was this crew who was the death of me.

FOURTEEN

Soapy's was packed. Like always, news had spread fast, and it seemed the whole town was here for his breakfast sandwiches. Roy, Johnna, and I stood in the line that snaked from the register and barista station in the center of the room all the way past the door on the side of the building, to the back wall.

Theresa took order after order, making coffee drinks and working the register as Soapy rushed in and out of the kitchen with sandwiches.

"They could use another pair of hands," I said. Then I saw Andy rush out of the door to the basement where they had their storage area. He wore a Soapy Savant shirt and an apron, and took a box marked HAZELNUT COFFEE FLAVORING behind the counter to Theresa.

"Looks like they have another pair of hands," Johnna said, eyeing me, like she was waiting for me to be jealous or something.

Why on earth would I be jealous that Andy had a job? If anything, I was relieved of the guilt I'd felt when I didn't need him anymore.

Who was I kidding? I missed having him around. I did feel a pang of jealousy that he was working somewhere else, but it was ridiculous! He couldn't work for me anymore, so of course he'd work for someone else. It was great that Soapy and Theresa had found someone reliable and hardworking like Andy. It was a perfect match for all of them.

"We can leave if it's going to be awkward," Johnna said.

"Why on earth would it be awkward?" I smiled and changed the subject. "Looks like they have three different kinds of sandwiches listed on their menu board. Which one are you getting?"

Fortunately, she turned her eyes to the board to read about the new offerings and dropped the subject of Andy. With him helping Theresa make coffee, the line moved quickly, and soon we were at the front.

Theresa gave us a warm and weary smile. "Good morning," she said. "It's nice to see you three. What can I get you?"

We ordered and moved down the line to where Andy was making our coffee. "I gave you an extra squirt of chocolate," he whispered to me, conspiratorially. Then he leaned in across the counter. I did the same, realizing he had something private to tell me. "Look back there." He jerked his head back toward the front of the cafe.

At a table by the window, Richard Banks sat with John Bridgemaker. My pulse sped. This was the break we'd been waiting for. This was proof. Granted, they might be old pals from back when Richard lived in the town, but Richard had a good decade, if not more, on John, so I was reluctant to believe they were childhood friends.

I nudged Roy and nodded my head toward our suspects.

"Lookie there," he said. "Think I'll go and say hello, see what the topic day jury is."

"Day jury?" Johnna shook her head. "I think you mean *du jour.* You're no international playboy, Roy, that's for sure."

He ignored her and, tucking his hands in his pockets, took a step to walk away before I grabbed his arm. "You can't go over there. Don't you remember how he kicked us out of the house — after insinuating that I could've killed Dixon and hid the ice pick?"

"I'll go," Andy said. "I have the perfect cover. I'll refill their coffee and eavesdrop at the same time."

"No," I said. "You can't do that. What if they complain to Soapy? I don't want you to jeopardize your job."

"Complain about coffee refills?" He smirked.

"Three bacon, egg, and cheese sandwiches," Soapy called, hustling up behind Andy. "I'll find you three when the line dies down to say more than good morning, but in the meantime — good morning!" He laughed and took off back into the kitchen.

"Two caramel cappuccinos!" Theresa called to Andy.

"We'll leave you to it," I said.

"I'll get the scoop and fill you in as soon as I get a break." He grabbed two cups and began packing coffee into a silver thing — some part of the fancy cappuccino maker.

"Let's sit as close to them as we can get," Johnna said.

"No tables up front, though," Roy said, steering us toward a table in the back corner. "This will have to do."

We settled in at our table, and I soon realized that all three of us were staring holes in Richard and John. "We need to take turns watching," I said. "We can't all do it at the same time."

"Yeah, Roy," Johnna said, "try being discreet."

224

"Look who's talking. You're about as discreet as a circus train pulling into to town."

"Oh, there goes Andy," I said, tracking his progress across the room with a coffeepot.

He came up behind John while he was talking and stood there for a moment, not interrupting. Then Richard looked up and smiled, pushing his cup toward the edge of the table to be filled.

Andy took his time. At least, he took as much time as he could to fill both cups, which wasn't much. The couple at the table next to Richard and John got up and left, giving Andy an excuse to linger, picking up napkins, empty sandwich plates, and coffee mugs. After he took the dishes into the kitchen, he came back with a cloth and wiped the table and each chair, slowly and methodically.

"I hope he's hearing some dirt," Roy said between bites.

"There's Claudia and Ethan James," Johnna said, "Elaina's great-niece and -nephew. They must be in town visiting. I think I'll go say hello." She hoisted her knitting bag over her arm and ambled off across the room.

"And there's Elaina and Dan," Roy said, watching the door.

225

Elaina had her arm hooked through Old Dan's and was practically dragging him across the room. I couldn't look at them without smiling. And laughing. That poor man was swept up in a tornado of polka dot–wearing force that he couldn't resist. Elaina had more energy than a woman half her age, and I should know, being just under half her age.

They made their way over to the table where Johnna had joined Claudia and Ethan James, who I believed were Elaina's brother's great-grandchildren. There were so many family lines to keep track of in Metamora that I often got them mixed up.

"There she goes, showing off her tea cozies," Roy said, shaking his head as Johnna pulled a couple knitted items out of her bag. "She'll try to hawk them for a buck or two."

"What's a tea cozy?" I asked.

"It's a sweater for a teapot," he said. "Supposed to keep it hot."

I didn't ask how he knew. I figured he got the whole rundown and probably even a demonstration from Johnna.

The Soapy Savant began to empty little by little as we finished our coffee. Andy finally got a break to come over and talk to us. He sat his own mug on the table and took the chair beside me. "What a morning," he said. "I feel like I just ran a marathon."

"The sandwiches were great," I said. "I think Soapy and Theresa are on to something."

"Enough chitchat," Roy said. "Spill it. What did you hear?"

"They're talking about Clayton's land," Andy said. "The Mound Builders' Association wants to buy it."

"I knew it," I said, my mind buzzing. "What did Richard say?"

"He was saying it would be difficult with Jason in prison."

"Did it sound like shady business?" Roy asked.

"Of course it's shady business," I said. "They're talking about making a deal without the land owner present. That's shady."

"How does this tie into Clayton's murder, though?" Andy asked.

"There are still a lot of moving parts," I said. "We're trying to figure it out."

"We're looking in the wrong place," Roy said, reaching for his flask. "This business isn't part of it."

"Don't be so quick to write it off." I took a sly glance toward Richard and John's table. "People have been killed for land before."

"What do you think, Andy?" Roy asked, eager to get someone on his side of the argument.

"I don't know. People are crazy, especially in this town. I have to get back to work." He hustled off without saying goodbye.

"Chilly," Roy said. "Seems he's still upset with you."

I looked after Andy, regretting the way our working relationship had ended. I did him wrong and had to find a way to make it up to him.

Dress shopping with Mia was one of my least favorite activities. The winter dance at the high school was a few weeks away, and Mia was on the court for the sophomore class. When I walked through the door getting home from Soapy's, she'd wrangled me into taking her to the prom and bridal store where all the girls bought their dresses.

"I told you," she said, shooting down the dress I held in my hand, "it has to be one of the colors for the dance — red, white, or black. It can't be blue."

"I don't understand why you all have to wear the same colors," I said, shoving the blue dress back onto the rack.

"All the girls on court have to match the colors of the theme."

"And it can't be long, but not too short, and not sleeveless, but not with sleeves either, and you want sequins, but not too many and not beads, is that right?"

"Yes." She flipped her hair over her shoulder and walked to the next aisle of dresses. "And I want the skirt to be puffy, but like layers of meshy fabric."

"Chiffon is what you mean. I think. Basically, we're on mission impossible." Where was Irene when you needed her? Probably bossing someone around somewhere. I followed Mia to the next row of dresses.

"I don't know why you won't just let me order one online," she said.

"Because you can't try it on. I'm not spending a bunch of money on a dress and waiting for it to show up just to find out that it doesn't fit, all before we end up here anyway."

She rolled her eyes. "I'm never going to find one. We need to go to Indianapolis. That's where Steph found hers. There's nothing in this stupid town."

"Before we lose our cool, let's go through all the dresses that they do have, okay?"

"I don't even know why I'm going. I don't have anyone to go with. I'm going to feel so dumb."

Mia never offered any insight about boys

and who she liked or who liked her. "You don't need a date to have fun at a dance. I'm sure you're not the only girl going without a guy. Isn't there a . . ." I spotted Robin walking into a fitting room. What in the world was she doing here?

"Hello? Earth to Cameron. Isn't there a what?"

"Oh. Uh, a group. A group of girls you can go with?"

I needed to find out what Robin was up to. Mia was going on and on about the dance, and I couldn't focus on what she was saying. A piece of the Clayton puzzle was right under my nose, I could feel it.

"Are you even listening to me?" Mia asked, crossing her arms in a huff.

"Of course I am. Let's just grab a few dresses and you can try them on. You never know what might look nice on."

"I haven't found any I want to try on."

I had to get Mia to the dressing rooms so I could run into Robin and find out what she was up to.

"Okay, listen. Don't ask me why, but I will take you to Indianapolis to shop for a dress if you pick one up right now and go try it on."

"No," she said, crossing her arms. "Why do you want me to try one on so bad?

What's going on?"

Mia had been involved in other investigations the Agency had undertaken. I didn't like bringing her in when I didn't need to, but it was clear she wasn't going to go along with my plan until I gave her a reason.

So I told her, and then asked, "Do you understand now why I need you to try something on?"

"All you had to do was explain why," she said. "I'm not a little kid, you know. I can help you."

Maybe she was right. She was a frustrating teenager, but when I treated her more like an adult, she tended to act more like one, too. It was hard to treat her like a grown-up, though, when she was freaking out about a dress for the winter dance.

She pulled a dress in her size off the rack. "Come on."

I followed her to the fitting rooms and took a seat on the nice plush chair by the mirrors to wait.

Robin was in the room two down from Mia. She'd been in there for about five minutes, and I hoped she would come out and take a look at herself in front of the big mirrors that showed different angles. Even if she didn't, I'd be sitting here when she came out.

The sales woman stopped in. "How's she getting along?" she asked. "Is the size okay?"

"I'm not sure she has it on yet," I said. "I'll let you know."

She knocked on Robin's door. "Can I be of any assistance?"

"I'd like to try this one in a smaller size," Robin said, tossing a black dress over the top of the door.

"Certainly," the sales woman said. "I'll bring it right in for you."

A minute later, Mia came out dressed in her jeans and sweater. "Didn't fit," she said.

"Mia," I said, and shook my head, pointing at Robin's dressing room door. "I'll find you something else."

Mia sighed and went back inside the fitting room. I hurried around the store, pulling a handful of dresses off the racks. I had to be sitting in that chair when Robin came out.

Rushing back, I knocked on Mia's door and pushed the whole armful in at her when she opened it. "Take your time," I told her. "I don't know how many things she's got in there with her to try on."

"Here you go," the sales woman said, handing the smaller-sized dress over the top of the door to Robin. "Let me know if you need anything else."

"I'd like this in purple instead of navy," Robin said, tossing another dress over the door.

"Right away." The sales lady whisked off to fetch the requested color.

At this rate, I'd be sitting here all night and Mia would have every dress in the store on and off again before Robin came out.

"Look at this one!" Mia said, bursting through the dressing room door. "It's perfect!"

Somehow I'd managed to grab a red dress with cap sleeves, a chiffon skirt, and a thin row of sequins around the middle. "It is perfect," I agreed. "Is the price perfect? Or will it send your dad through the roof?"

I stood and grabbed the price tag peeking out under her arm. "Not terrible. I think we can swing that."

Mia let out a cheer of excitement and jumped up and down. "Thank you, thank you, thank you!" She started taking selfies to send to Steph.

With that task accomplished, all I had to do was get Robin out of her fitting room to find out what brought her into a formal dress shop. Maybe it was nothing. But maybe it was something.

Mia changed back into her clothes and we paid for the dress, and Robin was still not coming out. I was almost ready to give up when Mia whispered to me, "Do you know which car is hers?"

"I'm not sure, but I know which cars were in Clayton's driveway, so I think I'd recognize it if I saw it."

"Okay, don't worry. I've got a way to get her out of the store."

We walked to the car — Monica's car — and Mia draped her dress across the backseat while I scanned the parked cars near us.

"I'm pretty sure it's that white Lexus," I said.

"Stay here. I'll be right back," she said and jogged back into the store.

A few minutes later, she came back out with Robin right behind her. "We saw the car speed away," Mia said. "I don't think it left a mark, but you should check."

Robin began to examine the front of her car. "I don't see any damage."

"Robin?" I asked, pretending astonishment. "Is this your car? I didn't see you inside. We just bought Mia's dress for the winter dance."

"Oh, this is Ben's daughter? Nice to meet you, dear," she said, shaking Mia's hand. "This is my car. I can't believe someone would hit it and dash off like that. I don't even see a scratch on it, though. What a relief."

What a good little liar Mia turned out to be. I wasn't happy about that, but it did get Robin out of the store. "What event are you shopping for today?" I asked her.

"The Native American Mound Builders of Metamora is having a little shindig tonight. Richard was just invited this morning."

"How nice," I said. "I didn't realize he was still close to so many people in town."

"Well, it's more of a business association," she said, stepping closer. "The president of the association has an interest in Clayton's property and offered to pay Jason's bail if we considered selling the land."

"Really? That's good news. Does Jason own the land? Does he want to sell it?"

"Richard's going to do some negotiating tonight before he approaches Jason with the offer, but it's worth a fortune to them."

"Wow," I said, tingling with the feeling that I was closing in on the motive I'd been hunting all along. "You and Richard could retire with that money. Travel the world!"

"I'm sure Jason would make sure we were comfortable, but it would be his money, of course."

"Of course."

"I have always wanted a house on the beach in North Carolina." She clenched her hands together in front of her, like she was hoping and praying her dream was about to come true.

The only person this deal didn't make rich was the one who was always bartering and trading for his livelihood. The one who might have, unknowingly, died for that land: Clayton Banks.

Fifteen

Sunday went by without incident. I washed laundry, cleaned the house, and did my best to clear my mind of solving murders. I had a well-deserved day off, which was good, because Monday morning dawned with Jason Banks knocking on my door.

I suppose it didn't *dawn* that way. Ben was already at work, Mia at school, and Monica at Dog Diggity. But it was still pretty darn early. Way too early for a suspected murderer out on bail to be on my doorstep. Not that there was ever a good time for that.

"Come in," I said, hoping he'd say no thanks, and that he couldn't stay long.

But he came in. "I know I'm the last person you expected to see," he said.

"I can't deny that." I held Gus back from jumping all over him but could do nothing about the twins. "Coffee?"

"No," he said, indulging Colby and Jack

as they sniffed his legs, curious about the dog they smelled. They'd never come across Ginger before. "I'll get right to the point. You said you'd find my father's killer. I need to you to find David Dixon's. I can't spend my life in jail for something I didn't do." He pulled an envelope out from his coat pocket. "I'll pay you in cash."

"Oh, good gravy. I can't take that. I don't know if I can even help you. I mean, I want to, but I don't know that I can."

"Because of our rocky start? Listen, I'm sorry about how I treated you. I didn't mean anything by it. I was —"

"No! No, Jason, not because of that. I know you were upset about your dad and didn't mean it. I can't promise that I'll figure out who killed Dixon or your dad. We're trying our best to figure it out, though." I took a breath. "Jason, what can you tell me about your mom?" I had a feeling he didn't know Robin was his mother, and if he did, I wanted to know if he'd tell me, or if I could tell he was lying.

Jason looked surprised. "What does she have to do with this?"

"I'm not sure she has anything to do with it, but I need all the information I can get. Does she live in the area?"

"My mom — the one who married my

dad and raised me — lives in Arizona now. But my biological mother is long gone."

"Is she still alive?"

He shrugged. "My dad loved her and she left him, that's all I know."

His answer could mean Robin or any other woman on Earth who he'd last known to be alive, whether yesterday or fifteen years ago. "You don't have contact with her?" I asked.

"She took off right after I was born. Left my dad and me and never looked back, so no, I've never had anything to do with her. If you think she had some reason to come back around now and kill him, you're way off. Her family gave my dad the house and told him to pretend he never met her. That's what he did for the last thirty-seven years. That's what both of us have done."

He had no idea that Robin — his uncle's wife — was his mother. Robin's family disowned the baby and paid Clayton off with that house and land! Now she and Richard knew its value and wanted it back. Their first obstacle? Clayton.

Their next obstacle? Jason.

"Oh, good gravy!" I shouted, making Jason take a step back from me like I was nuts.

"What?" he asked.

"I think you're in danger. I think whoever

239

killed your father did it to get his land. Now that land belongs to you."

He shook his head, eyes wild with confusion. "What do you mean? Why would someone kill my father for his house?"

"Not the house, the earth mound on his property."

"But I thought the police cleared John Bridgemaker and Paul Foxtracker? They aren't suspects."

"No, they aren't. Whoever killed your father wants to sell the land to John and Paul and make a profit — directly or indirectly."

He ran his hands through his hair, still shaking his head. "I don't understand. If they kill me next, the land would go to the state."

"And depending on the probate laws, your aunt and uncle could inherit the property," I said carefully, hoping it would sink in.

"Right," he said, "so how does that tie in to me being in danger?"

Who was I kidding? He wasn't going to suspect Robin and Richard of killing his dad, even though his dad and Richard had bad blood between them for decades. Why couldn't he see the connection?

"Just trust me," I said. "Don't eat anything you didn't cook and don't drink anything you didn't buy and pour. I don't care who it comes from, do you understand me? You told me your dad was poisoned, so don't let the same thing happen to you."

He held up his hands in surrender. "Okay. So what about David Dixon? I might not be poisoned, but how do I stay out of jail?"

"I think they're connected somehow, but I don't know how yet. I mean, it only makes sense. They were best friends. They died one day apart. Both murdered. That's not a coincidence."

"Then Starnes Buntley needs police protection. There was nothing my dad and David knew that he didn't. The three of them were inseparable and had been since high school."

"I think I need to have a talk with him, because you're right. He knows something, and I don't know if he even knows he knows it."

"What can I do? There has to be something."

"You're right. There has to be something in that house. Search through all of your father's papers and belongings. If you find anything at all that seems odd, call me."

"I'll do that right now. I'll be in touch." He turned and opened the front door to leave.

"I'll let you know what I get out of Starnes, if anything."

As soon as Jason was gone, I picked up the phone and called Betty to get Lana's phone number. "I just want to see how she's doing," I said, lying through my teeth. "I know Jason being out on bail has to be a relief for her."

Betty told me how kind I was to care, which made me feel like one of Gus's big piles of poo in the backyard. But this wasn't a time to dwell on feeling bad. Unfortunately, getting to the truth required telling lies, and it was easy thinking of one to tell Starnes to get him to see me.

Lana answered the phone and I introduced myself. "Betty told me how upset you were when Jason was arrested. I hope you're feeling better now that he's out on bail," I said.

"Of course," she said. "I know Jason didn't kill David. I don't know if they'll ever figure it out. I mean that show on television says the first forty-eight hours are critical and after that the chances keep decreasing."

"I'm positive that Ben and Sheriff Reins will find the person responsible," I said.

"Oh, sure. Yes, I'm sure. Do they have any leads?"

"Ben doesn't fill me in on the details no

matter how much I beg, but I'm sure they have a few."

"I bet it was a jealous competitor from his Olympic days," she said. "There was this one guy I remember from Florida. He was always coming in second to David in all the national competitions. Floyd Evans was his name. Ben needs to find him and haul him in for questioning."

A twang of desperation sounded in her voice. "I'll let Ben know," I assured her. "I was also wondering if Starnes was home."

"He is. Is there something you need him for?"

"Well, I couldn't help noticing what you had in your handbag at Clayton's wake. Betty told me Starnes had some on hand. I was wondering if I could stop by and pick up a bottle? Or maybe you two would be in town soon?"

"I'm sorry, I don't know what you're talking about."

"Lana, I already know the two of you make and sell moonshine. I'm not going to tell Ben or anyone. I only want to buy some."

"I didn't peg you for a dirty wife of a cop," she said.

"That's a bit harsh, don't you think?" I asked, taken aback.

"You're the one who has to face him every day," she said. "We'll be in town tomorrow for David's memorial service. His family had him cremated, you know. I don't think he would've liked that. He built his professional career in the snow and they end his days with cremation? That's not the way he would've wanted it."

"Did you know him well?" I asked.

"Of course I knew him well. He made a point to know everyone well. He was a busy body, a social butterfly. Always sticking his nose into everybody's business. Well, everyone loved him anyway."

"Someone didn't," I said, trying to keep her talking.

"Oh, I don't know. It's hard to say why anybody does anything they do."

"What time is his memorial? Do you think it would be okay for me to stop in? I don't want to intrude."

"His sister's holding it at his house at two in the afternoon. She'll be putting the house up for sale, so if you know anyone who might be interested, pass word along. I'm sure you're welcome to stop by."

"And you'll bring me a bottle of moonshine?"

"We always bring some with us."

"I'll find you there then."

"You know I've been questioned about Clayton's death? They think it was my blood pressure medication that killed him. How could it be me who poisoned him with something I lost? Just because it was the same brand, like I'm the only person on the planet who takes those pills. What reason on earth would I have of killing Clayton?" Her voice cracked. "I've known that man forever. He had a good heart. Sure he was rough around the edges, but once you got to know him he was the kindest soul you'd ever want to know."

"I'm so sorry," I said, sensing how close she and Clayton had been.

I didn't know they'd made a positive connection between her lost pills being the same kind they found in his system. My theory had been right then. Ben should be thanking me, not keeping me in the dark.

"It's okay. I just don't know how anyone could think I'd harm that man."

"Don't worry. Ben will get to the truth soon."

With my help, I didn't bother saying.

I hung up with Lana and considered her saying I was a dirty wife of a cop. Was I? Sure, I snooped around to help solve murders, and sometimes that meant I had to do things Ben wouldn't approve of. Was I going too far?

Even if I was, I couldn't back away now. I was getting close to figuring things out, I could feel it. All I needed was the puzzle pieces to fall into place.

Around noon, the Action Agency had assembled at my house. I had a feeling that even if we had world-class offices, we'd all end up congregating around my kitchen table with coffee and Betty's cookies anyway.

"What are these?" Roy asked, tapping a thin, dark brown cookie on the side of his plate.

"Ginger snaps," I said, getting out my notebook and pen.

"They're hard."

"Once you take a bite, they get chewy."

"My teeth aren't made of iron."

Johnna huffed. "Oh hush, and dunk it in your coffee,"

Roy did as she said and chewed slowly, considering the taste. "Nope," he said, dropping the cookie on his plate. "I don't like 'em."

"Well, they're my favorites," she said, snatching another from the cookie box in the middle of the table.

"They would be. They're hard and sharp

like you."

Johnna ignored him and took a bite.

"There's a memorial service for David Dixon tomorrow at two," I said, "and I'm going."

"Who isn't?" Roy asked, and took a swig out of his flask.

"You mean, you guys knew about it and didn't tell me?"

"Everybody knows," Johnna said, digging her yarn and knitting needles out of her bag. "It's not like there was a formal invitation sent out. Word spreads around."

"It didn't spread to me."

"You knew about it, didn't cha?" Roy asked.

"Well, yes, but I had to find out for myself when you two already knew."

"Didn't know we was your keepers," he mumbled.

I took a deep breath and moved on. There was no getting through to them sometimes. "Anyway, I called Lana and told her I want to buy a bottle of moonshine. I figured it would get me access to Starnes to ask him some questions."

"What are we for, then?" Roy asked.

"What do you mean?"

"Johnna and I have known those two a long time. We don't need an excuse, like

247

buying 'shine, to go up to him and start talking."

"Again," I said, "I didn't know you two knew about the memorial service and would be there. If you would've told me, I wouldn't have had to make this harebrained plan and get called a dirty wife of a cop!"

Johnna chuckled. "That's a good one."

"It doesn't feel so good," I said.

"Oh, you're the furthest thing from a dirty wife of a cop," she said. "You snoop around and ask some questions, big deal."

"Now I'm buying illegal moonshine."

She and Roy looked at each other and burst into laughter.

"Okay, so it's commonplace for everyone else around here, but not for me," I said in my defense. "And Ben wouldn't approve."

"He's never hauled his daddy into the hoosegow for buying 'shine," Roy said. "I can remember him and Jason stealing their dads' bottles and hiding out in the woods getting blitzed."

"Set a few trees on fire one time," Johnna said, pointing at Roy with a needle. "Remember that?"

He laughed and slapped his knee. "Bonfire got out of control on 'em."

"They were good friends then," I said, musing over the new information. "Wait,

248

Ben set the woods on fire?"

"Just once," Johnna said, going back to her knitting.

"Most cops have an interesting past," Roy said. "The good ones can think like a bad guy."

"Ben doesn't think like a bad guy," I said. "I mean, if he does, it's not because he is or ever was a bad guy."

"No, no, of course not," Johnna said. "He just had some fun in his younger years is all."

"Like most kids do," Roy added. "That Jason was trouble with a capital T. Ran up a list of offenses against people in town a mile long."

"Like what?" I asked.

"Let's see, there was the time he fired up Butch Landow's tractor in the middle of the night and ended up running it through his barn door. Put himself in the hospital that time."

Johnna lifted her needle. "Don't forget the time he broke into Soapy's and spiked the latte milk with 'shine. Half the town was sauced the next morning."

"He was in college then," Roy said. "Took that boy a long time to grow out of his ornery streak."

"What happened with him and Ben?"

"Ben became a cop, didn't he?" Roy said. "Can't be a delinquent and have a cop for a best friend."

"Their paths divided," Johnna said. "Then he arrested Jason for assault."

"Wait. What?" I said. "Assault? Who did he assault?"

"Richard," Roy said. "Popped his uncle right in the mouth. Took out a couple of teeth."

"So he's violent?"

"If you call punching a guy in the mouth violent, then I suppose he is."

"You don't?" I asked.

Roy shrugged. "Sometimes a man has to sock another fella in the nose. Happens."

But I wasn't sure. If Jason had a proclivity for assaulting people, then maybe he could've killed Dixon. "Did he ever assault anyone else?"

"Jason?" Johnna said, "Of course he did. That kid was getting in fights from the time he could make a fist."

"Only got arrested the once, though," Roy added.

"Interesting," I said, one piece of the puzzle coming together. "So that's what went on between them. How long ago was this?"

Roy leaned his head back, thinking. "Probably twenty years or so now. Ben was living in Columbus. Soapy gave him rights to police the town when he came home for visits. It was more a gesture from the town than a real thing, like a key to the city type of deal, but they honored Jason's arrest anyway."

"Wow," I said. "He wasn't even living here, or working as a cop in Brookville where they have jurisdiction over Metamora."

"That was Jason's legal argument," Johnna said. "Got him out of jail, too."

My mind reeled. "Okay, so why did Jason punch Richard?"

"Nobody knows," Johnna said. "Neither of them would tell anyone."

"I wonder if Jason somehow found out that Richard stole Robin from his dad," I said. "It makes sense. Jason, who was prone to that type of reaction, would've . . . well, reacted that way. He could've just pretended to me that he didn't know. Right?"

"Could've been that," Roy said.

Johnna nodded, resuming knitting a teapot cozy in the shape of a ski cap. It had a hole for the spout on one side, one for the handle on the other, one for the lid on the top, and the bottom was open to slide it over the pot. "Do those really work?" I asked her. It had

251

to be the most useless thing in the world if it didn't. They were cute though, I'd give her that. This one had yellow daisy appliqués that she was knitting on.

"I don't know," she said. "They're more a collectible item for people who collect teapots."

"A collection for your collection," Roy said, shaking his head.

"You'll be shaking your head when I'm rolling in the dough after I sell them at Canal Days next year," she said to him.

"People's bad tastes are no business of mine," he said.

The back sliding door opened and the dogs jumped up from their napping spots on the floor around the table. Ben came inside and patted their heads wading through the masses of wriggling fur and wagging tails to let them outside. "What's on the agenda today?" he asked, saying hello to Roy and Johnna and kissing me on the cheek.

"Telling tales about your younger years," Roy said.

"There can't be that many," Ben said, opening the refrigerator door.

"I don't know," I said. "Setting trees on fire is a pretty good story."

"It was one time," he said, smiling at the

memory. "Teenage boys aren't the smartest people on Earth." He let out a chuckle. "My mom wanted to kill me for that. She grounded me for the rest of the summer. Dad talked her down to three weeks."

"I can imagine Irene was devastated about what it would do to her reputation," I said.

"She was mortified."

"It was good ammunition," Johnna said. "Every time she got high and mighty on us, we'd remind her whose son set the woods on fire."

I could use some of that ammunition to get her to back down. Too bad Mia was the annoying-teenage type and not the delinquent-teenage type.

Who was I kidding? I'd take annoying over delinquent any day, even if I didn't have anything to hold over Irene.

"Speaking of Irene," Johnna said. "She still wants her cat competition to be held even if the rest of the Winter Festival doesn't get rescheduled."

"Oh, good gravy. First the dog sled guy and now her. Are the Daughters going to start picketing my house with their cat ear headbands on?"

Roy snickered.

"Don't worry," Ben said. "If they do, I'll turn my new snowblower on them."

"Good to know it has dual purposes," I said.

I couldn't see Ben turning his mother into a snowman, but it was nice to think about.

He made a ham sandwich, grabbed a bag of potato chips. "Anybody want anything to eat while I'm in here?" he asked. I'd told him about Roy and his food situation. "Roy? Sandwich?"

"I'm good, thanks," Roy said. "Actually, you got a baggie? I might take some of these cookies with me."

"You didn't like the cookies," I said.

"So they'll grow on me."

Ben got a plastic bag out of the drawer and handed it to Roy. "Johnna? Anything?"

"No thanks, Ben. I had one of Soapy and Theresa's breakfast sandwiches this morning."

"Okay then, I'll leave you to your Action Agency work." He grabbed a soda and headed into the family room to eat his lunch and watch the afternoon news.

Roy took a break for stashing cookies in his baggie, leaned across the table, and whispered. "Did you see his eye twitch when he thought about the fire? It brought Jason to mind. Bad blood there. Bad blood."

I hadn't noticed, but Johnna nodded. "Those two hate each other's guts," she said. "They used to be like brothers. Now they can't be in the same room."

If they'd been so close, I wondered why he'd never mentioned Jason to me before. All the memories he had of him seemed to be locked away tight. Inaccessible. Like he never wanted to revisit them.

But he had smiled when the memory first came to him, so maybe — despite the eye twitch — I could reunite my husband and his old best friend. Death had a way of bringing people together and making them put aside their differences.

Of course, if Jason really was a killer, I didn't want to rekindle the friendship he and Ben once had. Tomorrow after Dixon's service, I'd be one step closer to the truth.

Sixteen

Making a bright orange cast look somber for a memorial service was a challenge. A T-shirt wasn't appropriate, and none of my long-sleeved shirts fit over the cast. I had to cut off the arm of a black sweatshirt of Ben's and dress it up somehow.

"Wrap a scarf around it," Monica said, pulling a mottled black and grey one out of my closet. She wound it around my cast and tied it in a bow at my wrist. "There. Very nice."

"It's kind of strange looking," I said, waving my arm around. The ends of the bow fluttered.

"It's not traffic cone orange," she said. "Besides, it makes the sweatshirt look less . . . like a sweatshirt."

"True. Help me find some jewelry."

"Come in my room. I have something that will work."

I followed her across the hall. She pulled

a chunky silver necklace out of a drawer full of costume jewelry and hooked it around my neck. It had big, glittery gems studded through the fat squares of silver. "It's a bit much," I said.

"It dresses things up."

Next she wrapped a silver studded belt around my waist, cinching in the sweatshirt. "I really don't want to attract attention to my waistline," I said.

"It actually thins you out. This sweatshirt is shaped like a big box."

I let her go, making me up like a Christmas tree full of tinsel.

"There," she said, standing back to take a look at her handiwork. "You look nice. Nice enough for a memorial service at least." She strode back out of her room and into mine.

"Was that a compliment? I couldn't tell," I said, following her.

"Sit down and let me do something with your hair."

"I can do my own hair," I said, taking my hairbrush from her.

"One-handed brushing isn't doing your hair. Sit." She grabbed the brush again and pointed to the bed.

I sat on the end and waited while she retrieved the curling iron from the bathroom and plugged it in behind my dresser.

"I really have to crack this case today," I said, as she tugged at my hair with the brush. "I need a break. Something big that I can use to say, 'This is what happened.' "

"Want me to go with you? I'm pretty good at being the Daphne to your Velma."

"Why am I Velma?"

"Oh, please. Like you'd be Daphne."

"Gus is Scooby," I said.

"Which actually makes you Shaggy," she said, laughing.

"Your car's green. You own the Mystery Machine."

"In miniature."

We were both laughing like loons, more than the ridiculous conversation warranted, but Monica and I had a way of being silly together that only sisters could be. As an only child, Ben missed out on that connection between siblings. But, growing up he'd had Jason. I really wanted to prove Jason was innocent and bring them back together.

"You can come with me if you want," I told her. "Roy and Johnna will be there, so it'll be good to have another levelheaded person helping me."

"Those two know a lot, but sometimes I think they don't realize what they know can help. To them it's common town knowledge, but to you it could be the key to solving a

258

murder."

"They are great resources. They know everybody. But you're right, they don't always use what they know."

"I'll finish up your hair and get ready. Quinn's running the store today. He said I deserved a day off. Isn't that sweet?"

"So sweet it gives me a toothache."

"He's going to teach me how to train dogs, so we can do it together and merge our businesses. Isn't that a perfect plan?"

"Treats and training go together like a hand and a glove."

"Dog Diggity Training and Treats! I love that!"

"It has a ring to it. Which location will you keep?"

"Both, but we'll offer training here and treats in Connersville at his location, too."

"Is this after you come back from Ireland as married newlyweds?"

"I'm not getting married in Ireland! At least not without my matron of honor at my wedding. So if you get a call from me that I'm flying you across the Atlantic, I guess you'll know why. But, it's not going to happen. We want to take our time. We're talking about moving in together sometime in the spring maybe."

"You're leaving me? My kitchen will be

lonely without you in it cooking every day."

"It was only temporary, Cam. I need to find a place of my own eventually, don't I? Especially now that Ben's back home."

"Ben doesn't mind you being here."

"I know, but it's your house, you and Ben and Mia. You need time for your own little family."

"You know you can stay as long as you want."

"I know." She wrapped the last section of my hair around the curling iron. "That reminds me. Mom's coming to stay next weekend."

"What?" I said, jerking my head to look at her and nearly getting burned with the curling iron. "Why am I the last to know about this?"

"She only told me last night. She said to let you know she'd give you a call later this week."

"Ugh, that means I have to put up with her and Carl and their canoodling around town."

"Canoodling? You've been hanging around Johnna too much. You're starting to talk like her."

"Just go get ready to leave," I said.

"Mom coming shouldn't put you in a bad mood."

"It doesn't put me in a bad mood. It stresses me out. I need enough time to mentally prepare for her visits."

"I don't see why."

I sighed. "Because she tells you things. I get bombs dropped on me after the fact, like about her and Dad splitting up. Who knows what she'll tell me this time."

Monica glanced at her feet and turned to unplug the curling iron. "Give me twenty minutes and I'll be ready to go."

"Wait," I said, grasping her by the arm. "What do you know?"

"Nothing," she said, but she wouldn't look at me.

"Monica?"

"It's for Mom to tell you."

"Oh, good gravy. I don't even want to know, do I?"

"It's not bad. I mean, you'll see more of her now."

I stood up and gripped her shoulders to make her look at me. "She's moving to Metamora, isn't she?"

"Well . . ."

"Is she moving in with Carl Finch?"

"Uhhh . . ."

"Monica!"

"Yes! Okay? She's moving into Hilltop Castle."

"Is Carl going to be our new daddy?" This was a disaster.

"No! I don't think so. I mean, I don't know. She hasn't decided, but she accepted the ring while she's thinking about it."

"Of course she did. I suppose it's enormous."

"She said it's two carats."

"She wouldn't say no to that."

"I don't think she's going to say no."

"I thought she was just having a good time being single? What happened to that?"

Monica shrugged. "You know Mom. She can change her mind on a dime."

"Great. Maybe you two can have a double wedding."

Monica made a face. "No thanks."

The Cripps women all in one town again. Hold on to your hat, Metamora, you're about to get turned upside down.

Dixon's house already had a FOR SALE sign up in the front yard. Cars lined the street on both sides. The house was a small Cape Cod just outside of town heading in the direction of Connersville.

Evelyn Lister, Dixon's sister, welcomed us at the door, above which a pair of ski poles were anchored like a pediment. She looked like David, just female. I wondered briefly if they were twins.

Everyone from town was gathered in the adjoining dining room and living room. The table was piled with casseroles, and fruit and vegetable trays. A card table off to one side held beverages of all varieties.

I wandered around between the two rooms saying hello to people and taking in the framed photographs David had of himself in all of his Olympic glory. There were even framed newspaper articles, and a framed program from the Olympic trials featuring David on the cover. Every wall, every table, even the mantel over the fireplace was covered with his photos and memorabilia. I didn't know if he had decorated his home this way or if Evelyn had done it for the memorial.

Monica was chatting with Evelyn, hopefully getting some good information about who might have wanted to off her brother with an ice pick. Logic said that since the weapon was associated with ice and David competed in a winter sport, it had to be someone connected with the Olympics. One of his past competitors, maybe? But murder was seldom logical. At least the couple I'd solved in the past. I couldn't count anyone out.

Richard and Robin Banks stood in the

corner of the dining room chatting with an older couple I didn't know. I knew most of the two hundred residents of Metamora, and I didn't recognize them as people from town. I peered into the kitchen and saw a doorway people were going in and out of, so I followed along.

The doorway opened to a four-season room with windows on all sides. In every corner and mounted over each window were a pair of antique skis. David was definitely dedicated to his sport.

Old Dan and Elaina sat on a wicker loveseat on the far side of the room. I waved and Dan gave me a thumbs-up. Elaina flicked her fingers in a wave and kissed Dan on the cheek.

"Cam."

I turned my head to see Andy and Cass talking with Ed Stone, the TV newsman from the festival. "Hello," I said, joining them. "Good to see you again, Mr. Stone. Are you here personally or professionally?"

"A little of both, I'm afraid. With a story like this you can't pass up the opportunity to get something on film for the public."

"No, of course not." I glanced at Cass, but she was entranced by the local celebrity. "Where's your cameraman?" I asked, looking around for the man who had filmed the kids sledding at the Landow Farm when the festival's skiing competition went downhill.

"Right here," he said, taking Andy's wrist and raising his arm. "As of yesterday when I got a video sent to me in my email that this young man had filmed. Genius. I went to my producer and demanded that we hire him immediately."

"You're kidding!" I said. "Andy, that's wonderful!" I grabbed him in a big hug.

Andy grinned ear to ear. "It's amazing. I'll be working in my field. I never thought I could stay here in town and use my skills to make a living."

Cass beamed. I could see the relief wafting off of her. She didn't have to worry that he'd leave town (and her behind) for a career. He wouldn't have to make a choice.

"I'm so happy for you," I said to them both.

I caught sight of Lana and Starnes walking through the doorway. "Excuse me," I said, and hurried over as fast as I could without seeming too obvious.

"Hello," I said, and held out my hand to Starnes. "Good to see you both again."

"And you as well," Starnes said. "Is that husband of yours around? I haven't seen him in ages."

I didn't know if he really wanted to see

Ben, or if he was scoping the place, hoping the cops weren't around so he could sell his moonshine. "He's working today."

"Solving this case, I hope," he said. "Such a shame. Who would do such a thing?"

"I have a feeling we'll never know," Lana said. She smiled and took a deep breath. "Well, Cameron, I have a bottle for you in my handbag. It's ten dollars."

"Should we do this right here?" I asked, glancing around. "Right now?"

"Just about everyone here will be buying a bottle from us today," Starnes said. "Nobody minds."

Lana set her enormous leather bag on a pedestal table by the wall, moving aside another framed portrait of David in his ski helmet. Bottles clinked together inside. "I have them wrapped in brown paper," she said. "So it's discreet."

"Yes, very discreet," I said under my breath.

"What are you doing?" Monica asked, coming up beside me.

"Making a purchase. What are you doing?"

"Maybe the same," she said. Then she whispered to me, "This house is bank owned. I can get it for a steal."

"Bank owned?" I whispered back, but

Starnes had turned around and started talking to Jefferson Briggs, and Lana was busy unzipping her good times bag of hooch. "I didn't know Dixon was broke."

"Apparently, he was. Evelyn said the bank officially foreclosed last week and put the house on the market yesterday." She looked the room over from top to bottom, grinning. "This is the perfect room for Isobel. She'd love it out here. There's so much sun that comes through the windows. I'd put her bed right over there." She pointed to where Cass, Andy, and Ed Stone were standing.

"That reminds me, Andy has a new job. Go ask him about it."

"Are you trying to get rid of me?"

"What gave me away?"

"Fine, Velma. Do your thing."

She walked away, and Lana turned around. "Ten dollars," she said.

"Right." I swung my bag around to my front and opened it. It was hard to get into it and dig around one-handed. I pulled out what I thought was my wallet but ended up being a portable battery for my cell phone. "Do you mind holding this for me?"

I handed it over to Lana and dug back in. "It's impossible to find anything in this bag. Do you have that problem with yours?"

"Not really," she said watching me with a fascination.

My pain pills rattled around somewhere in the depths of my bag. "I thought I took those out of there." I grabbed another object that turned out to be a business card holder and handed it to her. "Third time's a charm."

She shook her head, unconvinced.

I stuck my hand back in and found it. "Voilà!" I yanked my wallet out and my pain pills fell to the floor, clattering together in their bottle. "Good gravy."

I bent to pick them up and realized they weren't my pain pills. It was a rectangular pill holder that was shaped like a container of Tic Tacs, but it sure wasn't mine. In black marker the name *Lana Buntley* was written on one side. I held it out to show her.

"You have my pills!" she shouted, snatching them from me. "My blood pressure pills! You have them! You killed Clayton!"

"What?!" My heart rattled around in my rib cage much like those pills had been rattling around in my purse. Every eye in the room was on me. "No! I don't know how those got in my bag!"

Starnes grabbed me by the arm. "Someone call the police!"

Monica's eyes were as big as dinner plates.

She stood frozen beside Andy and Cass, who were equally as astonished.

Ed Stone hailed his cameraman.

I fixed my eyes on Old Dan. "Tell the bees I'm going to jail."

Seventeen

Ben sat in a metal folding chair outside my jail cell in Brookville four hours later. He leaned the chair back against the bars and stared ahead of him at the sea foam green wall. That was the color that Irene accused me of painting Ellsworth house; my house was nowhere near sea foam green. "Tell me again how you didn't know those pills were in your bag," Ben said.

"I know it sounds crazy, but you've lived with me for enough years to know my purse is always a mess. I can't ever find anything inside it. I have no idea what's in there. The Holy Grail could be hiding out in there for all I know."

"This is bad, Cam. You heard the judge at the bail hearing. We're looking at a possible murder charge. At the very least you're getting obstruction of justice. You concealed a murder weapon whether you knew it or not."

He leaned forward and put his face in his hands.

"I'm sorry. I know this makes you look terrible. You're a police officer and your wife is in jail. You know I didn't do anything, though. There has to be a way to prove it."

"There is. Tell me how those pills ended up in your bag."

"I don't know! I wish I did."

"Think, Cameron," he said, whipping around to face me. "Think!"

I closed my eyes and pressed my fingertips against my lids. My head was starting to pound. "Someone framed me. That's the only thing I can think of."

"Who would frame you, and why? Who has it out for you?"

My nemesis came to mind. "Mr. Mustache. The crossing guard who stands at the corner."

Ben blinked a few times, like he couldn't understand what I was saying. "Why would a crossing guard have it out for you?"

"I kind of gave him the finger once."

Ben let out a soundless chuckle through his nose. "I don't think that would make someone want to frame you for murder."

"He was there — at Clayton's house the day of the festival — the day Clayton was killed. He asked me what I was doing there

271

when I went with you that morning. Or maybe I asked him. Whatever. Either way. He was there, and I was there, and he had to have been the one who put those pills in my purse."

"And how did he get the pills in the first place? Are you suggesting he's the person who killed Clayton? What was his motive? Did they even know each other?"

"Everyone knows each other here, Ben! And motive is your job. You're the cop." I slumped back on the bench.

"I think you're grasping," he said.

"I don't know who else hates me enough to set me up as a murderer."

"Do you really think it was the crossing guard?"

I sighed. "No. I guess not."

"Who then?"

"I don't know. I remember hearing a rattling sound in my bag though, before I even broke my arm. I didn't think it was pills. I figured it was mints or candy or something. I guess after I broke my arm I just thought it was my pain pills."

"Okay, good. That's progress. So how long ago was it? Before you broke your arm but after Clayton died. That was only Friday to Monday, Cam. It was sometime over the weekend when you heard it. Think about that time frame. What did you do after Clayton died but before you broke your wrist on Monday?"

I ran back through that time. "Well, I went with you to Clayton's, where the ski course was being set up. I talked with John there. I talked to Soapy on the phone and we decided we needed to find a new location for the ski competition. At home the Action Agency and Soapy all met to regroup. We ended up begging Phillis to let us use her farm. Let's see, after they left, what did I do? Oh, you and Mia came home. Mia had a game to cheer at that night." Then it hit me hard, like a piano falling on my head. "Ben!" I jumped up off the bench and darted to the bars of the cell. "I went over to Clayton's to talk to Jason. That's when I slipped on the sidewalk and my bag up-ended and everything fell out. I grabbed as much as I could in the dark from the flower beds between those stupid pricker bushes and shoved everything in my purse. That pill box must have been in the bushes at Clayton's house!"

Ben reached through the bars, grasped the sides of my face and pulled me forward to kiss me. "I'm going to talk to Reins. I'll be back."

■ ■ ■ ■

I sat in the cell for what seemed like forever. What if it didn't matter how I got the pills in my bag? What if Reins, or the judge, or whoever decided if I was a murderer, didn't believe me? Maybe I needed a lawyer. Sure, the arresting officer was my husband, but I should still have legal representation.

Monica and Quinn were let through the locked door at the end of the hall and ushered to my cell by a short, stocky officer I'd never met. One of Reins's Brookville PD sidekicks. "Ten minutes," he told them, and left them standing outside my cell bars.

"Ben told us everything," Monica said.

"We know you're not a murderess," Quinn said in his Irish lilt.

"I called Mom," Monica said. "They're getting you out on bail."

"Who is? Who's they? Who has that much money?" My bail was set at five hundred thousand dollars. Even a bond would cost fifty grand.

"It's not so much a *they,* actually," she said.

"Finch," I guessed.

She nodded. "He'd do anything for Mom."

My stomach twisted. I was happy for Mom. She found a great guy. Carl was really smart and had a good head on his shoulders. If he loved her, then I had nothing to complain about. I just wasn't ready for a stepdad, and I wasn't ready to owe him five hundred thousand dollars for bailing me out of jail.

"She's on her way here," Monica said. "She left about an hour ago."

That gave me about an hour and twenty minutes to mentally prepare.

"Carl will be here in a few minutes," she said. "He's putting up bail next door at the courthouse and then he'll come over here. Luckily he knows someone in the clerk's office; usually they're closed by now."

"Okay. That's very nice of him. I appreciate it."

"You sound like a robot."

"It's been a long day, Mon."

"How are we going to find out who did this? Do I get the Action Agency together? Do we meet in the morning?"

I nodded. "They'll be in our kitchen in the morning whether I call them or not. You don't have to do anything."

"Everyone in the room was stunned when you were arrested."

"Was it on the news yet? That cameraman

was right in my face."

"Don't worry. I think Andy took care of that."

"What do you mean?"

"All I know is he offered to help the cameraman set up because they were in a rush to start filming before the cops got there. After they took you away Andy told me he was taking care of it, and you would never be on the news as an accused murderer."

"Oh, good gravy, he's going to lose the job he just got all because of me being stupid and not knowing what I'm lugging around inside my purse."

"No, if he loses his job it's because he saved a friend the pain and humiliation of being publicly branded a murderer on TV."

"Same thing," I said. "It all comes down to being my fault."

The door at the end of the hall unlocked and squealed open again. Carl came through with the police officer who'd escorted Monica and Quinn in. They reached my cell and the officer unlocked it. "You're free to go. You're not to leave town. Officer Hayman is responsible for your adherence to the terms of bail."

Carl patted him on the back and thanked him. Carl knew everyone.

"Thank you," I said to Carl. He was smiling like he couldn't be happier to spend that much money.

"You're more than welcome. I'm happy to be able to do it for you."

I took in his nicely styled gray hair, his tan slacks, button-down shirt and loafers and couldn't help smiling myself. My mom was a lucky woman.

"We can put a payment plan together," I said. "I'll give you an amount each month until . . ." I let my words drift off. Carl was shaking his head.

"You must've forgotten that you saved my life," he said. "If I was dead, I'd certainly never have met your mother. My life alone is worth the amount of your bail, but with her, it's worth more than anything. We're even."

"No, I couldn't accept it."

"It's done," he said, holding up a hand. "I'll hear no more about it. As long as you appear at any court hearings, the money will be refunded. Minus some fees. Now, let's get you home. Your mother is on her way there now."

Well, if I was going to have a second dad in my life, Carl wasn't such a bad one to have around.

Mom paced around the family room with a wineglass in her hand. Her heels made little indentations in the carpet. Carl sat in the antique wingback chair watching her every move. Even though it was nearly ten o'clock at night, Monica and Quinn were in the kitchen making popcorn. Ben sat next to me on the couch with Colby and Jack nestled between us, and Mia was laying on the floor holding Liam with her head resting on Gus.

We were all lost in thought, wondering how I was getting out of this mess.

"Clearly," Mom said, "this Lana woman poisoned him. She dropped her pills as she was leaving." She took a sip of wine and paced some more. "Clearly," she repeated.

"We've already questioned her," Ben said. "There was nothing we could arrest her on."

"But now we have pills and her name on them," Mom said, "found at the scene of the crime."

"Allegedly," Ben said. "I believe Cam, of course, but a judge has to believe her. Lana will be questioned again tomorrow. If there's anything we can hold her on, she'll be arrested, too. But that doesn't clear Cam."

"This is just ridiculous," Mom said.

"I'm going to visit Judge Hendrix in the morning," Carl said. "Put your mind at ease, Angela."

She paced to his chair and kissed the top of his head. "How will I ever thank you for what you've done?"

He patted her on the bottom and shrugged his eyebrows up and down. My stomach went queasy. I didn't need to see that. Now I knew what Mia felt like when Ben and I first started dating. There's just something odd about seeing your mom with a man who isn't your dad, I don't care how old you are.

Monica and Quinn came in with two huge bowls of popcorn. "Cheddar cheese flavor and regular butter flavor," Monica said, setting them both on the coffee table.

Mia sat up and grabbed a handful of the cheddar cheese flavor. Gus put a paw on her leg, silently pleading for some. Liam wasn't that polite. He jumped up and ate a piece from the pile in her hand.

"Liam!" she shouted, and he ran toward me and Ben and hid under the couch. "You runt," she said.

Roused, Colby and Jack bounced off the couch and started circling the table.

As soon as this was over, all the fur balls

were going to training. Or maybe Ben could take them while I was in prison for the next twenty-five years to life.

"Outside!" Mom shouted. "Let's go!" She rounded them up and headed for the back door.

"Do I look good in orange?" I asked, holding my cast up to my face.

"You're not going to prison," Ben said, taking my hand and lowering my arm. "Have some popcorn and try not to worry."

"I've called my attorney in New York," Carl said. "He's flying in tomorrow."

"Wow," I said. "You have an attorney in New York?"

"When you collect antiquities from all over the world, you have to have the best."

"I suppose so."

"Thank you, Carl," Ben said. "I can't thank you enough for all you're doing to help us."

"I'll do whatever is in my means and require no thanks. We'll all do everything we can to get Cameron out of this."

The doorbell rang.

"Who would be coming over this late on a Tuesday?" Monica asked.

"Please tell me they aren't here to take me back to jail," I said, ready to run and hide in the attic.

"No," Ben said, "but let me find out who it is."

He treaded through the hallway and I heard the front door open then Soapy's voice. The two of them came through to the family room. "There's our convict," Soapy said, teasing. "I figured you hadn't had anything to eat, so I brought over some food."

"Thanks, Soapy, that's so thoughtful." I stood and took the bag and set it next to the popcorn. "Come on in and sit down. Can I get you anything to drink?"

"No, no. I just wanted to bring something by. I don't want to disturb you."

"You're not disturbing us," Ben said, gesturing for Soapy to sit on the loveseat. "I'll get you a drink."

"Okay then," he said and sat down. "But I won't stay but a few minutes. So what's going on? How did those pills end up in your purse?"

I told him the story. "So we have to hope the judge believes me."

"Hmm . . ." Soapy tapped his lips. "Or we get Lana to confess."

"How do we do that?"

"I'm not sure."

"That's the crux of it, isn't it?" Carl said.

"It is, but we've known Starnes and Lana

long enough to find their weaknesses. We'll think of something."

"Not the moonshine," I said. "It seems everyone already knows about that."

"It's not enough of a charge to stick. Not enough to confess to murder to get past. That's like trading in a Mercedes for a broke-down Ford. But there must be something we can use as leverage," Soapy said.

Ben handed Soapy a glass of tea. "I can't let the whole town get involved in police business," he said.

"I'm the mayor."

Ben shrugged. "Works for me." He sat back down beside me. "We can use all the help we can get."

Mia opened the bag of food Soapy brought and took out some tortilla chips and salsa. "Homemade," Soapy said. "There are some sandwiches in the bottom."

"This salsa is my favorite," she said, digging in. I'd never seen Mia so eager to eat, she was either starving or nervous.

The doorbell rang again. "We're popular tonight," Monica said.

"I'll get it," Quinn said, gesturing for Ben to stay seated.

"It's probably Theresa coming for me," Soapy said.

"Where is that daughter-in-law of mine?"

Irene's shrill voice called from the hallway.

"We're in here, Mom," Ben shouted.

Irene rushed in with Quinn and Stewart on her heels. "How on earth did you end up arrested for murder? Do you have any idea how many phone calls I've gotten this evening?"

"Sorry?" Good gravy, I was the one thrown behind bars! I was so sorry she was inconvenienced by it.

"I'm going to grab a drink," Stewart said. "Got anything strong in this house? And I don't mean wine. Hello, Carl. Angela. Soapy. Nice to see you. Quite the houseful."

"I'll help you," Monica said, following him into the kitchen.

Mia hopped up and hugged her grandma.

The doorbell rang for the third time. "It's Grand Central around here," I said. "Probably Andy and Cass. I'll get it."

I padded in my socked feet to the door. Ben followed. "It's getting claustrophobic in there," he said.

I opened the door and was shocked to find Jason Banks standing on the porch. He looked at me, and then Ben. "I have something to show you," he said, and held out a stack of envelopes.

"What are these?" Ben asked.

"Blackmail letters to my dad."

"Blackmail letters?" I asked. "From who?"

"David Dixon."

EIGHTEEN

Ben and I waited until everyone left to read the letters. Jason didn't stay, and we told everyone that it was Will Adkins from next door stopping by just making sure everything was okay since he saw so many cars over at our place.

We sat in bed reading by the light from the lamps on our nightstands. What we found out was that Clayton had been having an affair with Lana, and David found out about it. "He needed money," I told Ben. "His house was foreclosed just last week."

"So he blackmails his best friend? I'm not defending what Clayton did, but blackmail is never okay."

"And they both ended up murdered," I said.

"So if Clayton doesn't pay up then our primary suspect in Clayton's murder is David. It would seem that David killed Clayton and then someone killed him." Ben shook his head slightly, studying one of the letters. "I don't like that theory. It doesn't make sense."

"If Clayton didn't pay, David wouldn't kill him, he'd go to Lana next and blackmail her."

Ben sat up a bit more. "Maybe he was blackmailing her, too. Double the money. She killed him and stashed the ice pick under Clayton's couch to frame Jason. Jason has the letters and the ice pick. Weapon and motive."

"What if it *was* Jason? Weapon and motive."

Ben frowned. "And he had the perfect opportunity to deflect the accusation to Lana and get himself off the hook. She was sitting where the weapon was found, and then he finds these letters."

"It's got to be one of them, but that still leaves us in the dark about who killed Clayton if not me, which we know it wasn't me."

"Would Lana kill Clayton if she was having an affair with him?"

"I don't think so. You should hear the way she talks about him. I thought it was because they were old friends, but maybe she really loved him."

Ben let his head fall back against the headboard. "Who would kill him then?"

We both looked at each other, the answer dawning on us both at the same time. "The husband," I said.

"Of course."

"Starnes found out and killed Clayton," I said.

"And Lana took out David before he could tell Starnes."

"Do you think either one knows what the other has done?"

Ben set the letters on his nightstand and turned off his light. "I don't know, but there's one way to find out. Ask. She's being called back in for questioning tomorrow."

"And you think she'll tell you, just like that? You're the police. She isn't going to tell you anything."

"So how do we find out then?"

"Ben, leave it to me."

"No way. No. We're dealing with murderers, Cameron. Two of them."

"Then you can be my backup, okay? But let me talk to her before your interview, woman to woman. She has nothing to lose. I'm still the one who had the pills. I'm the one who got arrested. Anything she tells me one on one is just hearsay. I can't prove it even if she admits it. But, if I'm wired and you hear it, too, that's different."

"This is dangerous. I don't like it."

"I know you don't, but we're doing it. I'm not going to jail for the rest of my life. The question is when and where. Once we know that, we get me out of this mess."

I turned off my light, snuggled down next to him, and put my head on his shoulder. I knew he would never be comfortable with my solution, but I also knew I was right. It was the only way.

Walking the dogs in the early morning while the snow fell in soft, wispy flakes was one of my favorite things. Gus snapped at them, eating them like a gourmet dessert falling from the sky. Snowflakes melting on Colby's nose made him sneeze, and Jack liked to try to tunnel in the snow banks built up by the plow. Liam wanted no part of going for walks in the snow and preferred to take as short of trips as possible two feet outside the back door with Isobel, who also wasn't up for walks in cold weather.

Again, like it had every time I'd passed the canal in recent days, my mind wandered to Metamora Mike. I honestly didn't know how the town would fill the duck-sized hole that he would leave if he didn't turn up again.

There were very few people out, but those I did see walking from their house to their car or taking out the trash would glance my direction and away again, pretending they didn't see me. Did they think I was guilty of murdering Clayton? Or did they just not know what to say? Either way, it was discomforting. How could my neighbors even consider that I'd do such a thing?

Of course, the real killer had to have been someone Clayton knew to get close enough to poison him, so why not believe it was me?

I had to clear my name. There had to be a way to confront Lana Buntley privately, while wired with a microphone. I would get her to confess if it was the last thing I did. And it very well could be. My life was over if I was sent to jail for the rest of it.

Mom and Monica were at Dog Diggity setting up new display stands that Mom had bought and surprised Monica with. She'd always been Mom's favorite and always would be, especially seeing as how only one of us was accused of murder. They were probably all giddy planning their weddings as they screwed the displays together.

I took a deep breath of the cold, fresh air

and willed my head to clear. I couldn't worry about Mom right now. Or Monica, or Carl, or anyone but myself. Except maybe Andy.

I took my phone out and dialed his number. "Hey," I said when Andy answered. "You don't think I killed Clayton, do you?"

"It's me you're talking to, Cam. How could I think that?"

"Just making sure. Anyway, Monica said you told her not to worry about the footage the cameraman shot of my arrest. I don't know what you did, but thank you a million times. Did you get fired before you even started?"

He laughed. "No. I'm not that careless. He had no idea what happened to it. Somehow the whole thing got wiped out."

"Well, whatever you did, you're the best. I owe you one or ten or a thousand."

"It's what friends do. You did it for me. You didn't stop looking for the real killer when I was in jail for Butch's murder. Consider this repayment."

I'd never even thought of that. First Carl says he's paying me back by posting bail, and now Andy says his . . . whatever he'd done to that film was repaying me. "I didn't do it so you'd repay me, you know."

"I know, but I'm glad I could."

When I got off the phone I felt better. Andy and I were friends again. He had a good job that he wasn't going to lose for helping me, and he was staying in town. Something was going right with the world at least.

The dogs and I walked past the gazebo in the center of town. Spook the cat sat on one of the benches inside. He watched us pass with an air of being above all of us. Cats were such strange animals. One minute they were cuddly and affectionate and the next aloof and distant. You never knew what you were going to get. And Spook was definitely mysterious, even for a cat. The way the dogs never seemed to see him make me wonder if he really was a ghost.

On our way back, we strolled past the grist mill. Frank was shoveling the walk while Old Dan sat in a rocking chair on the side porch whittling. "Good morning. What are you making?" I asked him.

"A duck call."

Something about Old Dan trying to call back Mike made my heart clench. "We have to find him," I said.

"We will."

"You sound pretty sure of that. Has he done this before?"

"No."

"Then how do you know we'll find him?"

"Bees told me," he said, and winked.

Roy, Johnna, Anna, and Logan were waiting in the kitchen with Monica when I got home. "Shouldn't you two be in school?" I asked Logan and Anna.

"You were arrested for murder last night," Anna said. "We're helping you figure this out."

"This is more important than a perfect attendance record for twelve years," Logan said. "Thirteen if you factor in kindergarten, but who's counting?"

"No! Logan, you blew your attendance record for me?"

"You'd do it for me," he said.

"I would. You're right. Thank you for being here." I wanted to give my brainiac boy a hug but knew the gesture wasn't something he'd appreciate. He wasn't one for affection, but honesty and getting the job done would be the way to show him. "Let's get to work then," I said.

I pulled out the letters. They passed them around, reading while I made a second pot of coffee and Monica ran down to Betty's for a fresh batch of cookies.

Roy whistled. "I didn't see this coming."

"I'm not surprised," Johnna said. "I've

always known that Lana was a loose goose."

Logan was taking notes as he read. Anna bit her nails flipping through one of the letters, like the drama was too much to take.

"Is this appropriate for young eyes?" Roy asked, nodding toward Logan and Anna.

"We're eighteen," Logan said. "Legal adults."

"I suppose if you're old enough to see an adult film and serve your country, you can read about adultery in a bribery letter." Roy sat back, shaking his head. "What's this world coming to?"

"Oh stuff it, you old crow," Johnna said. "They had adultery in the Bible."

"So, what do you think?" I asked. "I mean, what do you think this has to do with Clayton and David's deaths?"

"Only everything," Anna said.

"It's highly probable that the contents of these letters was the motive for both murders," Logan said. "Give me ten minutes and I'll have a statistical analysis."

Roy scratched his head. "We don't need no statistics. Since the beginning of time men have been killin' other men over the womenfolk. It's the way of things."

"Are you saying Starnes killed Clayton for sleeping with his wife?" I asked.

"Of course he did. It's clear as day."

"How do we prove it though?"

"We don't. We have to get him to admit it."

"How do we do that?"

"Only way I can think of is to put Lana in danger somehow."

Johnna banged her hand on the table. "We aren't going to put Lana in danger!"

"I don't mean physical harm, woman. I mean make him think she's going to jail."

"Good gravy, that's it!" I shouted. "I don't need to confront Lana. I need to confront Starnes while Lana's being questioned today and make him think she's getting arrested."

"Yes!" Roy pointed at me. "That's what I meant."

"Okay, let's figure out how I get him somewhere that I can confront him. Originally, Ben was going to wire me so I could talk to Lana and he'd be listening, but I think we should scrap that." Well, Ben hadn't actually agreed to it in the first place. "I'm going to need you guys to hear what Starnes says since Ben will be busy interrogating Lana at the police station."

"I'll record the audio," Logan said. "I only need to be close enough to hear his words. One room away would do fine."

The phone rang. I saw Ben's number on

the caller ID. "It's Ben. Stop talking about this." I waited for them to zip their lips before I answered.

"Cam," he said, "I told Reins about the letters. I'm on my way home to pick them up, so if you want to read through them again, do it now."

"You what? Why did you do that?"

"It's evidence. I can't withhold it."

"Why do you have to be a cop?"

"There's something else. Reins is bringing Jason back in. It's too coincidental that he had —"

"The weapon and a motive?"

"Exactly."

"I don't think he did it, Ben."

"Neither do I."

"I'll see you when you get here." I hung up and scurried around the table collecting the letters. "He's taking these to Reins. They're evidence, so he has to hand them over."

"Take 'em," Roy said, pushing one across the table to me. "We've seen enough."

"Jason's been taken back into custody with these letters as evidence of his motive."

"Doesn't help that the ice pick was under his couch, either," Roy said.

"Caramel apple cookies," Monica called,

strolling through the door. "Warm from the oven!"

"I could eat a dozen of those," I said.

"That's why I bought two dozen." She sat them in the middle of the table and we dug in. I filled her in on the letters and Jason.

While we talked, the dogs nudged around our legs, and dove under the table and back out snuffling around for crumbs. Colby lifted his head and looked at me with a white feather stuck on his nose. "Where'd you get that?"

"Probably a bed pillow," Johnna said. "Might even be from my bag. Charlie tore one of mine up the other day."

"That's probably where it came from then," Roy said. "I'm sure it is. Where else would it be from?"

Johnna scowled at him.

He took his flask out and threw back a swig.

The two of them behaved so odd sometimes. They had a love-hate relationship, that was for sure. They loved to hate each other.

"Dogs," Logan said. "That's it. Clayton had a dog, right?"

"A Chow Chow named Ginger," I said. "Why?"

"That's how we get Starnes alone while

Ben's talking to Lana at the station. Jason's in jail. We tell Starnes he needs to pick up Ginger and take care of her. He'll do it for his departed best friend, if only for appearances."

I shook my head. "Clayton's brother and his wife are staying at his house. It won't make sense if they're taking care of Ginger."

"Starnes doesn't need to know that. We get those two out of the house somehow and tell Starnes that they went back home."

I looked around the table at the others. "It might work," I said.

"Might," Roy agreed.

"I think I know how to get them out of the house, too. I need to call John Bridge-maker."

Not that I was keeping tabs, but since Carl and Andy had brought it up, I figured John might do me a favor for getting him out of jail when he was a suspect in Butch's murder, too. Not that I was planning on prefacing it that way. But I hoped it was in the back of John's mind when I asked him to lure Richard and Robin Banks to lunch to discuss the sale of Clayton's property.

NINETEEN

One thing we hadn't figured out was how we were getting into Clayton's house. Roy had made the call to Starnes saying he heard Jason had been arrested again, and since Richard and Robin had gone back to Lexington there was nobody to take care of Ginger. Starnes readily agreed to come and meet him here to get the dog.

"Break the lock, not the window," Logan told Roy, who was trying to wedge a tire iron between the upper and lower panes on one of the windows at the back of Clayton's house.

"You guy are ridiculous," Anna said, taking her school ID from her pocket. She ran it between the back door and its frame, right where the lock would be beside the doorknob, and the door popped open.

"How did you do that?" Logan asked.

"I'm always locking myself out of the house, so my dad taught me," she said.

"Where'd he learn it?" Roy asked.

She shrugged and went into the garage.

Roy looked at me and raised his eyebrows. "Don't turn your back on that one," he whispered.

"Girl after my own heart," Johnna said and wandered in after them.

"I just hope there's no alarm on this house," I said.

Roy scoffed. "Metamorans don't have alarms on our houses. The only reason the door's locked is because Richard and Robin aren't from around these parts anymore."

"I guess big city life got them to lock their doors."

Roy shook his head. "Darn shame. Now our young girl has to go and break in like that."

Ginger started barking. "Now that's an alarm," I said, hurrying inside and through to the house.

Anna was feeding Ginger some bacon from her coat pocket, and Logan was already setting things up in the bedroom closest to the living room. "You guys have this handled," I said, catching sight of Johnna on the sofa taking out her knitting.

"It might be our last investigation with the Action Agency, so we wanted to take the lead on things," Anna said. "Prove ourselves before we head off to college in the fall."

"You guys have all summer. We'll have more to do before you leave."

"Probably not another murder, though. At least I hope not."

"We've had enough of those," Roy said. "Let's hope we get through this day without another one."

"You look about as nervous as a dog passing tacks," Johnna told him.

"We'll be fine," I said. "This will take maybe ten minutes. Why don't you look around and make sure everything's secure?"

Roy wandered around searching — for what I didn't know. But I'd given him a mission and he was going to do it. When he started opening cupboards, I knew he was searching for something else. Food and booze. "Don't take anything, or Richard and Robin will know someone was in here," I said.

"Do they take inventory before they leave the house?" He snapped back.

Anna hurried into the bedroom to see if Logan needed anything. Ginger followed her. I strode to the front window to keep watch for Starnes.

I ran through our plan in my mind. Richard and Robin were with John. Lana was with Ben at the station. Jason was tucked away in a cell for now. Starnes would be by for Ginger. And none of them would be the wiser that they were being set up.

Anna came out of the bedroom with Ginger at her side. "You better take the bacon, or she'll want to be with me in the bedroom the whole time."

"Good idea." I took the bacon, thinking that I should've brought some dog treats with me.

I gave Ginger a little bit to let her know I was the one with the goodies now, then I sat down on the couch with Johnna and stroked Ginger's fur. "Roy, come sit down and wait with us. He'll be here any minute."

Roy sat in the chair that was most worn. I figured it had been where Clayton usually sat. It faced the TV and had a matching ottoman with indentations where feet would be propped. Ginger left my side and padded over to Roy. She placed her head on his lap and whined a little.

"Now, now, girl," he said, petting her head. "I know it's hard. You'll be okay."

I passed him the bacon, even though he didn't seem to need it. "She likes you."

"All women do," he said and gave me an exaggerated grin.

Johnna snorted but didn't bother looking

up from her knitting.

I heard the crunch of gravel outside. "I think that's him." I stood and got a look out the window. His truck was parked and the driver's door was opening. "He's getting out."

"Help us out, Ginger," Roy said, getting up. "Do whatever you can. We want to find your daddy's killer." He took long strides to the front door and opened it. "Hey there, Starnes," he said. "Come on in. She's ready for you."

"Good to see you again, Roy. I'm glad you called me. I'm happy to take her back home with us." Starnes stepped inside and stopped, seeing me. "I thought you were in jail," he said.

"I'm out on bail. I didn't kill Clayton."

"What are you doing here?" He looked to Roy. "What's this about?"

"It's about your best buddy, Clayton," Roy said. "Come on in. We've got some bad news that you don't want to take standing in the doorway."

"Bad news?" He came inside and Roy closed the door.

"Sit down, Starnes," Johnna said, patting the sofa beside her. "Roy, get him something to drink."

Roy gladly hustled from the room. Starnes

looked around, like he was on *Candid Camera,* which he kind of was, except it was the audio-only version. Reluctantly, he took a seat on the couch. "What's this about?"

"I wanted you to hear it from friends instead of a cop," I said.

"You killed Clayton. You're no friend of mine."

"I don't know if you believe that or not, but that's not what this is about."

Roy came back in with a glass of clear liquid. Water or moonshine, I couldn't be certain. He handed it to Starnes.

"Tell me what's going on," he said, looking up at Roy.

"You know Cameron's husband is the law in this town, right? So she hears some things."

"And?"

Exasperated, Johnna took up the reins. "And Lana's being taken into custody for killing Clayton," she said. "It was her pills. She dropped them on the sidewalk after she poisoned him. Cameron only had the bad luck to pick them up after she fell and dumped everything from her handbag into the bushes."

"That's not true," he said, and I thought we had him. But then he said, "She's in for questioning, but she's not being held. She's not a suspect."

"She is," Roy said. "That's why we met you here. You can take the dog if you want, but that was just a ploy. We wanted to break it to you easy."

"This can't be happening. How did those pills end up there?"

"Where?" I asked.

"In the . . . handbag you were carrying."

I'd almost trapped him.

"Unless you killed him," he added.

"Johnna just explained how they ended up in my bag."

"But that's not — it can't have happened that way."

"Why not?" I asked.

"Because it doesn't make any sense. Lana didn't have a reason to kill Clayton."

"Neither do I."

He took a sip of his drink and winced a little. It was moonshine. Good job, Roy, maybe it would loosen his tongue.

"So where *did* Lana lose her medication?" Johnna asked.

"Who knows?" he said. "They fell out of her purse somewhere."

"But they couldn't have fallen out here?" I asked. "When was the last time she was here before Clayton died?"

"We hadn't been in town for quite a

while," he said.

"And she wouldn't come on her own?"

His eyes narrowed for a split second and he took another drink from his glass. "Why would she?"

"The police seem to have evidence that puts her here more often than that," Johnna said.

"What evidence is that?" he asked.

"The same that put Jason back behind bars."

"The murder weapon that was under this sofa?"

"And the letters," Roy said.

"What letters?"

What if he didn't know? What if we were about to break it to him that his wife was having an affair with his dead best friend? "I think we should just all take a break, okay?" I said. "The police will explain the evidence. The important thing for you to understand is that Lana is being taken into custody right now as we speak."

"Then I need to get down there." He got on his feet and headed for the door.

"Wait!" I shouted.

He stopped and turned around. He wasn't admitting anything and he didn't believe us about Lana. This whole plan was going right down the toilet.

"We know it was you," I said. "It's just the four of us here. We know you took your wife's pills and poisoned Clayton with them because he was sleeping with Lana."

Starnes didn't say a word. His expression didn't even falter. He stood there and stared at me. He wasn't going to say one word in front of Johnna and Roy. They were witnesses. If it was just the two of us, he might. He could always say that I was lying to get myself off the hook, and I'd have no proof otherwise. Except I would, but he didn't know it.

"Johnna, Roy," I said. "Would you mind waiting for me in the car?"

Johnna's eyes shifted around, like this was some kind of signal and she forgot her next line. Roy stood frozen to the spot, looking to the door and back at me, like it was a test.

"Go ahead," I said. "I just want to talk to Starnes alone for a minute. That's it, just one minute is all I need."

Both of them puttered out the door, looking back a time or two.

"Okay," I said. "Listen. It's just you and me. I think we both know I didn't kill Clayton, but I can't prove that. If the judge believes me then maybe I have a chance. But if I go to jail for the rest of my life for killing a man, then I want to know the truth. For peace of mind and that's it. If you tell me the truth, there's nothing I can do with that information anyway. Even if I told someone, it's my word against yours. A murder suspect out on bail against the man who was Clayton's best friend? Nobody would believe me."

I leaned against the wall in the foyer and waited for him to reply. What I'd said was from the heart. I needed the truth just to hear him say it. If, by chance, he confessed and Logan didn't get it recorded, it would bring me peace knowing the truth even if I rotted behind bars. Not knowing would be worse.

"You're right," he said. "You can't prove anything. But I'm not taking any chances." Starnes reached under his coat and pulled a gun from his waistband.

I held up my hands and took a step or two backward.

"I'll shoot you first, then go out and get Roy and Johnna."

"You won't get away with it," I said. "Richard and Robin know you were coming to get Ginger. I'm sure they got word to Jason. Lana knows, of course. Maybe she'd keep it a secret that her husband is a serial killer."

"Serial killer? Hardly."

"Well, how many does it take to become a serial killer, anyway?"

"More than four, surely," he said.

"But there are only three of us here."

"Three. I meant three."

"Starnes, you killed him, didn't you?" I asked. "It's got to be hard to carry that around with you. He'd been your best friend for your whole life. And then he and Lana . . . and you did what you thought you had to do. I can't do anything with that information, so get it off your conscience. It has to be a terrible burden."

The gun shook in his hand. "Don't tell me how it happened," he said. "I know how it happened."

"Did you know about the letters from David? Did you know he found out and was blackmailing Clayton?"

"He was blackmailing Lana! Not one cent leaves our bank account that I don't know about. I found the letters when she was at church one Sunday morning."

"And you confronted Clayton about it?" I eased back another couple of steps.

"He denied it at first, but I told him there was no reason to."

"And you couldn't shoot him, could you? He was your friend. So you did it another way. A way that was less violent?"

Starnes shook his head. "I wouldn't shoot him. Not Clay."

"How did you know Lana's medication would counteract his own like that?"

"You can find everything on the Internet."

"Did you put it in the moonshine so he wouldn't taste it?"

"You could put a gallon of motor oil in my 'shine and not taste it."

"It's that strong?"

"Best around."

"So it must have taken about twelve hours or so to actually kick in, I guess."

"Seems like it. Knowing Clay, he spiked his morning coffee, though."

"That would do it."

He lowered his gun. "It does feel good to get that off my chest. Now I have a question for you."

"Okay."

"Does five murders make me a serial killer?" He raised his gun again. "Because I know you have someone in this house listening to every word I say, and neither one of you is making it out of here alive."

"What makes you say that? I sent Johnna and Roy outside. You can see them in the driveway sitting in my car."

I started to sweat and get chills at the

same time. There was only so many near-death experiences a woman could take, and I wasn't all that sure I'd walk away from this one.

Starnes waved his gun back and forth. "You go ahead and open all the doors in each room. I'll be right behind you."

I headed for the four-season room first. Since it was in the back of the house, I hoped it would give Logan and Anna enough time to sneak out the front door. "Nobody in here," I said, standing in the middle of the room.

"Keep moving." Starnes waved his gun around again.

Since we walked through the dining room and kitchen to get to the four-season room, there was nowhere left but the hallway with the bathroom and bedrooms. I started for the bathroom.

"Skip it," he said, walking by and looking in through the open door. "Nobody's in there.

The next door was the bedroom where Logan and Anna were set up. I grabbed the doorknob, but the door was locked. "This one's locked," I said, and took a step to move on to the second of three bedrooms, eager to get him moving along.

"How'd it get locked if there's nobody

inside?" He pointed the gun at the doorknob and fired off a few rounds. I jumped out of my skin and my ears rang. For the limited amount of time I had left, I wouldn't be able to hear a thing.

Starnes kicked the door open, and I imagined Anna and Logan huddled together inside, but they were nowhere in sight. "Open the closet," he ordered.

I did.

It was empty other than an old suit hanging on the rod and some Christmas decorations.

Where had Anna and Logan gone? The bed sat too low to hide underneath. There was nothing else in the room other than a bureau of drawers.

I looked around carefully. Both windows were locked, so they didn't sneak out that way. Maybe they had made it out the front door and locked the bedroom to give them even more time while Starnes tried to figure out where they were inside. That would be a brilliant idea that Logan would automatically do without even giving it much thought.

"There," Starnes said, jerking his gun toward the corner of the room. "See where the carpet comes away from the wall. Lift it up. I forgot that was down there."

What was down where?

I crossed the bedroom and lifted the carpet to find a door in the floor, the same kind you'd find on a ceiling leading up to an attic. "Open it," he said.

I grabbed a metal ring and pulled, lifting the trap door and praying Logan and Anna weren't down there. Unfortunately, they were.

It wasn't a large area, only a crawl space where the two of them were huddled. "Come on out," Starnes said. "I didn't expect three. One more notch for my gun holster, I guess."

"What will you do then?" I asked. "Go on the run for the rest of your life?"

"I'll have to, won't I?"

Logan and Anna climbed out of the crawl space. "It's too late," Logan said, stepping in front of me and Anna. "The police are on their way." He held up his laptop. "I sent them the audio file I recorded. They have your confession."

"There's no sense in killing us then," I said, trying to get back in front of Logan. "You need to get out of here before it's too late to get away."

A resigned look came over his face. "Go!" he shouted. "All of you get out of here!"

He didn't have to tell us twice. We bolted

out of the bedroom, through the living room, and out the front door. It slammed and locked behind us.

"What about Ginger?" I yelled. "Starnes, let Ginger out the garage door!"

There was no response from inside. I had a bad feeling I knew what he was planning. I didn't think Ben and Reins would take him out of that house alive.

"Cameron!" Roy shouted. "Get over here!"

Logan hooked his arm through mine and led me swiftly down the sidewalk to the car with Anna right in front of us. "We called the police," Johnna said. She held up an old cell phone. "I keep it in my knitting bag for emergencies."

We heard the sirens then. They seemed to approach from all sides. The first on the scene were from Connersville, followed by Brookville and Metamora One.

Ben grabbed me by the arms and said, "Get home and don't leave." Then he was off with his brethren in blue, surrounding the house.

I had no compulsion to stay. It wouldn't end happily, even if it did end with proof of my innocence.

TWENTY

A week and a half had passed. The ringing in my ears had passed. Ben's anger at me might never pass.

"We make a good team," I said to him on Saturday morning over breakfast, "admit it."

He stabbed a piece of sausage with his fork. "We're not a team in the sense of having badges and going up against men with guns and working in a professional capacity investigating cases." He chewed while staring at me with piercing eyes.

I waited until he swallowed to ask, "Husband and wife?"

"Then yes, we're a great team."

At least we had that going for us, and I hadn't screwed everything up.

"You better hurry up and get ready," he said, checking the time. "The dog sled man will be here in a half hour."

It had been a long and harrowing few

weeks for Metamora. Starnes had taken his own life rather than being sent to prison for the rest of it, and Lana broke down when she heard the news about her husband's death. She confessed to killing David Dixon. She'd had no idea Starnes killed Clayton, though. She took Dixon's life to keep him from telling Starnes about the affair and to stop the blackmail.

The first night of the festival, as she walked casually by one of the ice sculptures, she sneaked one of the artist's ice picks into her handbag. Then she lured Dixon to the parking lot near the port-o-potties by sending him a text message saying she had money to give him. Instead she gave him a one-way ticket to his own funeral.

When Ben let Jason out of his cell, they shook hands and looked each other in the eye. It wasn't a major breakthrough, but it was a good first step.

I got up from the kitchen table and headed upstairs to get ready. Mia was in the bathroom fixing her hair, and Monica stood beside her putting on makeup. "You two share a mirror well," I said.

"Soon we won't have to share at all," Monica said, putting her blush brush down. "I got a call from the bank, Cam. They accepted my offer for Dixon's house!"

315

"Really? Congratulations!" I gave her a hug while she bounced up and down on her toes, too excited to contain her energy.

"Isn't that awesome?" Mia said, "I can't imagine owning anything."

"You will," I said. "Someday." She was the heir to Ellsworth House, so she was standing in what she'd someday come to own.

"You're happy about this, right?" Monica asked.

"Of course I am. It's going to be strange without you here, but you'll be right down the road. We'll see each other all the time."

"Every day," she said.

It still wouldn't be the same, and I felt a little lonely already thinking about Monica leaving. But I was very proud of her and happy for her. First she opened a business and now she was a homeowner and soon she and Quinn would get married. She'd found everything she'd ever wanted here in Metamora.

"Mom's moving in today," she said.

"Today? I thought it was next Saturday."

"Nope. It's today. The moving van gets to Hilltop Castle at one o'clock."

"It's surreal that both of you will be living here in town. Seems like only yesterday that I was living here and felt alone. Then we snagged Mia and you and now Mom. This town is like a magnet."

"Maybe it's not the town," Monica said. "Maybe it's you and Ben."

"Well, for you and Mia, maybe, but it's Carl for Mom."

She laughed. "I'll give you that one."

"Cam!" Ben shouted from downstairs. "Roy and Johnna are coming up the sidewalk!"

"I'm hurrying!" I called back.

Those two had been hovering around me like a swarm of bees. Having a gun drawn on me made them overprotective. But it was a gesture I understood. They were the older generation in this town, and it was their job to look after the younger ones. That's how it worked here in Metamora. We all looked after each other like one big annoying, loud, crazy, loving family.

Phillis let us use Landow Farm for the dog sled races with one stipulation: the dogs wouldn't leave any stinky presents on her property for her to find. Bobsled Bob assured me that his drivers picked up after their teams.

At the starting line, Andy and Cass were in the far lane, with Soapy and Theresa on the inside. Next was Brenda and Will, and in the nearest lane the team hadn't shown up yet.

"We'll start in two minutes, if you want to find replacements," Bob said.

"Who's missing?" I asked.

He glanced down at his clipboard. "Carl Finch and Angela Cripps."

"What? My mother's in a dogsled race?"

Carl's Mercedes came flying into the lot and parked. He and Mom rushed out of the car and over to us. "We're here!" Mom said, out of breath.

I just stared at her, speechless.

"Take your place on the sled," Bob said, pointing to their team and driver.

Monica came up beside me. "She's happy."

"I can't believe she's on a dogsled. In heels."

"She's laughing. Look at her."

I could count on one hand the number of times I'd seen my mom truly laughing. I tilted my head. "She is happy, isn't she?"

"It's all worked out for the best."

It had. I could get used to seeing Mom smile and laugh like that.

It was a shotgun start. My body involuntarily jolted at the sound. Andy and Cass took an early lead, until Cass somehow lost her boot and they had to stop to retrieve it.

Soapy and Thersea were neck and neck with Will and Brenda. Mom and Carl seemed to have a lackadaisical team of dogs who would rather sniff the ground and each other than race. In the end, Will and Brenda edged out Soapy and Theresa by a nose.

The next event was the hockey game that Soapy had put together. Ben and I walked hand-in-hand over to the frozen canal that had been cleared and squeegeed to a shine. Soapy had logs brought in and placed on the banks to sit on, like bleachers. He even screen printed some T-shirts big enough to wear over winter coats, with team logos on them. It was the Metamora Mikes versus the Metamora Mills.

Soapy captained the Mikes while no other than Roy captained the Mills. "I hope he hasn't been drinking," I said to Johnna, who'd taken up roost on the front-row log and had her knitting out in her lap. "He'll break his neck out there."

"That old goat has a few tricks left up his sleeve. Don't you go worrying about him."

Ben was on Soapy's team along with Quinn. Roy had Frank and Andy. The rest of both teams were made up of the older generations who I feared would break a hip. "This is a bad idea."

"Those men have been living their lives

longer than you've been living yours. They know what they can and can't do anymore."

"I know. I just worry," I said, watching my father-in-law take the ice.

At least Carl Finch was smart enough to sit this one out while cuddling with Mom and sipping cocoa from a thermos.

"I didn't know Quinn could ice skate until he signed up on Soapy's team," Monica said, sitting down beside me and handing me a paper cup of hot coffee from the Soapy Savant.

"Ben and I went once when we were first dating, but he didn't strike me as proficient enough to play hockey. This should be interesting."

"Every man in town is going to end up on the couch with his back out," joked Monica.

The game started. Roy took a fall during the first half and sat on the ice taking a swig from his flask before he got back on his feet. Ben took a spill and went face first into the snow on the bank. Stewart grasped his hand to help him up and ended up falling down beside him.

After a while they determined it would be best to only play until the first team scored and call that a win. A half an hour later, when every member of both teams had

320

found themselves down on the ice at least twice, they just called it a tie.

They all came off the ice smiling, laughing, and patting each other on the back.

Everyone wandered inside the grist mill, where old Dan had graciously given in to Elaina's pleading and hosted the Kittens in Mittens event.

Two long tables had been set up with name tags taped to the edges. Elaina held her white Persian, whose hair seemed to waft out into the air every time it moved. Since she'd taken to giving the cat a new name each week, I wasn't sure which name tag was her cat's.

Irene had recently adopted a Devon Rex cat, a very regal, if small gray male with a Napoleon complex. She named him Ellsworth. He looked like a drawing of a gray alien that people swear they see, with his big eyes and round ears. He sat bored, licking his paw, at his spot on the table.

In the end the whole thing had to be called off because of Spook, who took it upon himself to steal the grand prize: a four-ounce tuna steak. He swept down from the rafters, snagged it out of a tray of ice where it was displayed with fresh parsley all prettily, and disappeared with his loot.

Irene was steaming mad and called for

Soapy to do something about the stray cats around town. *Stray* was a loose description of Spook since he was always housed and fed somewhere. Inside I cheered him on, but outwardly, I stayed stoic to the whole scene.

At the end of the one-day make-up Winter Festival, everyone agreed it was a blast. Next year we'd make it a whole weekend event. As long as nobody was murdered.

Ben, Soapy, and I were the last to leave the festival after cleaning up and making sure we had volunteers to haul the logs away from the banks of the canal.

"Nice job, Cam," Ben said, as we strolled across the bridge toward home. "I know it wasn't the original plan, but you came through and gave the town a great day."

"Me and the Action Agency," I said. "They do so much to help this town. I think I'd like to do something for them."

"Well, speaking of that, I've got something to help Roy. I told Reins and the other Brookville officers that one of our veterans was having a tough time and we all pitched in. I got a gift card to the Save-A-Lot. It should last him all year."

"You did? That's the nicest thing I can imagine. Thank you for doing that for him."

I stopped and put my arms around him. "Do you have it on you? Let's go give it to him now!"

"I do. It's in my wallet. Let's go on over."

"Where you two headed?" Soapy asked out his car window. "Doesn't look like the direction of home. Can I give you a lift?"

"Listen to this," I said and told him what Ben had organized.

"Get in, I want to go along and see his face."

We got in the car and buzzed down the road to Roy's trailer home. Johnna's motorized scooter was sitting beside his car. "What are they cooking up?" Soapy asked. "It has to be something. If any two people in town are coconspirators, it's those two."

Another car pulled in right behind us. Jason was behind the wheel and Ginger sat in the front seat. We all greeted him when he got out of the car, with Ginger hopping out behind him.

The door to the trailer opened and Roy stuck his head out. "What's this then? A congregation? The church is down that way." He nodded down the road, then saw Jason and Ginger. "You, I was expecting," he said.

Jason stepped forward and handed Roy a leash and a bag. "I have her food and water bowls in here, and her toys and blanket. One of Dad's slippers."

"Good man. Now, don't you worry about her. I'll take care of her. Me and this girl took to each other like a duck to water," Roy said, patting Ginger on the back.

"Are you leaving town?" Ben asked Jason.

"I am. I accepted an offer from John Bridgemaker for Dad's house. I can't have pets in my apartment, so Roy's agreed to take Ginger."

"Well," Ben said, scuffing the snow with his boot, "it was good seeing you again. Take care of yourself."

"You, too. Thanks for figuring out it was Lana. I have no desire to spend the rest of my life behind bars."

Ben chuckled. "You get older and start to realize you're not invincible anymore."

Smiling, Jason nodded. "We never really were."

Ginger, who'd wandered inside the trailer, began barking to beat the band, and next thing we knew out the door flew Metamora Mike wearing a tea cozy like a sweater.

"How'd he get in there?" Roy said, sheepishly.

"Roy!" I yelled. "Have you been hiding Mike all winter?"

"Well," he said, shrugging, "with Johnna.

Not just me."

"Now don't you go blaming this on me, you old bat!" Johnna said, popping up beside him in the doorway.

"Why'd you think I was taking home those terrible cookies the other day?" Roy asked, screwing up his face. "Johnna's been giving me her old bread and chips. It's too cold to expect an old duck to live in a horse stall by the canal."

"Why didn't you tell anyone? The whole town is afraid he's dead or finally got enough brains to fly south."

He stood up a little taller, trying to look dignified. "I have a reputation, you know. I can't let people think I'm soft."

"A reputation as a drunkard," Johnna added.

"So you're not going hungry?" I asked. "We thought you needed money for food and that was why you were asking everyone for scraps."

"I told you I didn't need nobody's pity. Why won't nobody ever believe me?"

Ben looked at me and shrugged. "I suppose we can donate the grocery card to a veterans organization."

"I'm just glad Mike's back."

We watched as Ginger chased Mike, trying to give him a good sniff. Mike honked and waddled, trying to flap his wings that stuck out the sides of his tea cozy sweater as he made his way down the side of the road toward the canal.

"Go tell the bees Mike's back in town," I said.

Ben glanced over at me and smiled.

It was a good life we had in Metamora.

DOGS DIG BANANA BONANZA DOG TREATS

2 cups oat flour
1 1/2 ripe bananas
1 egg

Preheat oven to 375° F. Mash one of the bananas. Slice the remaining 1/2 banana into 12 thin slices. Mix oat flour, mashed banana, and egg. Scoop 1/4 cup of dough into ball and flatten slightly. Place onto a lined baking sheet. Press one banana slice into each treat. Bake for 20–25 min. Allow to cool completely and store in an air-tight container. Makes one dozen.

DOG DIGGITY'S BEGGIN' BAGELS

3 cups wheat flour
1/2 tsp. baking powder
1/4 tsp. baking soda
1 Tbsp. dried parsley
5 slices crumbled bacon
1/2 cup shredded cheese
1 tsp. vegetable oil
1 cup water

Preheat oven to 350° F. Mix flour, baking powder, and baking soda. Add parsley, bacon, cheese, oil and water. Kneed until dough is formed. Roll dough into 1–2-inch balls. Poke the bagel hole through each ball with the end of a wooden spoon or spatula. Bake on lined baking sheet for 45–50 minutes. Allow to cool completely. Refrigerate in air-tight container. Makes two dozen.

ABOUT THE AUTHOR

Jamie M. Blair (Ohio) is the *New York Times* bestselling author of young adult and romance books, including *Leap of Faith* (Simon & Schuster, 2013) and *Lost to Me* (2014). You can visit her on Facebook.